91110000016835

D0293912

HELEN FIELDING

Bridget Jones:
The Edge of Reason

Retold by Anne Collins

MACMILLAN READERS

INTERMEDIATE LEVEL

Founding Editor: John Milne

The Macmillan Readers provide a choice of enjoyable reading materials for learners of English. The series is published at six levels – Starter, Beginner, Elementary, Pre-intermediate, Intermediate and Upper.

Level Control

Information, structure and vocabulary are controlled to suit the students' ability at each level.

The number of words at each level:

Starter	about 300 basic words
Beginner	about 600 basic words
Elementary	about 1100 basic words
Pre-intermediate	about 1400 basic words
Intermediate	about 1600 basic words
Upper	about 2200 basic words

Vocabulary

Some difficult words and phrases in this book are important for understanding the story. Some of these words are explained in the story, some are shown in the pictures, and others are marked with a number like this: ...³. Words with a number are explained in the *Glossary* at the end of the book.

Answer Keys

Answer Keys for the *Points for Understanding* and *Exercises* sections can be found at www.macmillanenglish.com/readers.

Contents

BRENT LIBRARIES	
91110000016835	
Bertrams	14/09/2010
	£8.50
BRBAR	

A Note About The Author

Helen Fielding was born on 19 February, 1958, in Yorkshire in the north of England. She went to Wakefield Girls' High School and then studied English at St Anne's College at the University of Oxford. She worked for many years in London as a newspaper and television journalist, travelling to Africa, India and Central America. During this time, she wrote her first novel, *Cause Celeb*, published in 1994, which was set in Africa.

In 1995, Helen was asked by a British newspaper, *The Independent*, to write a newspaper column about herself. But she preferred to write about a fictional woman instead. So she created the character of Bridget Jones – a single career woman in her thirties whose main goals in life are to lose weight and attract a man.

Many single women in their thirties identified[1] with Bridget. Nobody had written about their lives in such an honest and funny way before. Bridget was not a beautiful film heroine[2], but a likeable, ordinary woman with real-life problems. Helen's column became very popular and was turned into a book, *Bridget Jones's Diary*, which was published in 1996. The sequel – the book which follows it – *Bridget Jones: The Edge of Reason* was published in 1999. Both books became best-sellers and have been made into highly successful films.

Helen Fielding is a very funny writer. In 2003, she was listed in *The Observer* newspaper as one of the fifty funniest people in British comedy. Many other comedy writers are her friends.

Helen has written another novel, *Olivia Joules and the Overactive Imagination* (2003), and she co-wrote the screenplays for the two Bridget Jones films. Today she works full-time as a novelist and screenwriter, and lives in London and Los Angeles.

Bridget Jones was a great success because Helen Fielding wrote about a subject which not many other writers had written about before. She showed women that there is nothing wrong with being single. They shouldn't worry about it, but should enjoy life and have fun. Some people think that Helen Fielding is Bridget Jones and is writing about her own life. But this is not true. Helen says she wrote *Bridget Jones* as a way of making herself laugh. Many of the ideas in the book have come from her friends. She has succeeded well in making many other people laugh too.

A Note About The Story

The Edge of Reason continues the story of *Bridget Jones* and is equally warm and funny. At the beginning of the novel, Bridget is in a very different situation from the previous book. She is now going out with her perfect man, Mark Darcy. But, as is usual with Bridget, things do not go smoothly with the relationship. A threat soon appears in the form of the beautiful, slim and intelligent Rebecca, who is determined to steal Mark away.

In addition, Bridget has problems with Gary, the builder who promises to do extension[3] work on her flat. Many of the memorable and funny characters in *The Edge of Reason* also appear in *Bridget Jones's Diary*. These include Bridget's best friends, Shaz (also referred to as Sharon and Shazzer) and Jude, Bridget's mother, her mother's friends Una and Geoffrey Alconbury and Richard Finch, Bridget's awful boss at the TV company Sit Up Britain.

But there are new characters too, such as Wellington, the African who Bridget's mum and Una bring back from their holiday in Kenya. The most dramatic part of the novel is when Helen Fielding takes Bridget on a disastrous holiday to Thailand. One of Fielding's great gifts is that she is able to create comedy from situations which are not funny at all. She is also a wonderful observer of people and a great caricaturist[4]. She focuses on certain types of people and brings them to life in a very funny way. For example, Charlie, the young Assistant Consul[5] in Bangkok, is typical of the kind of wealthy and well-educated British men who work in such jobs.

Helen Fielding said that she got the idea for *Bridget Jones's Diary* from Jane Austen's famous novel, *Pride and Prejudice*. Although *Pride and Prejudice* was published in 1813, there are many similarities with *Bridget Jones's Diary*. In a similar way, *The Edge of Reason* has parallels with Jane Austen's last completed novel, *Persuasion*, published in 1818, after Jane Austen's death. In *Persuasion*, the heroine, Anne Elliott, is persuaded by her friends to break off her relationship with the man she loves deeply, Captain Wentworth, just as Bridget is persuaded by her friends to leave Mark Darcy.

Some characters and scenes in *The Edge of Reason* are very similar to scenes in *Persuasion*. For example, Rebecca, Bridget's rival[6], jumps into a shallow lake and hurts her foot. This mirrors a scene in *Persuasion* when Louisa, Anne's rival, refuses to listen to advice and falls on her head and hurts herself. In both books, the heroines, Bridget and Anne, win the admiration of the men they love, Mark Darcy and Captain Wentworth, following the sensible way in which they deal with the situation. Helen Fielding has even used the name of a character from *Persuasion* in *The Edge of Reason* – Giles Benwick, who in both books ends up with the heroines' rejected rivals, Rebecca and Louisa.

Pride and Prejudice and *Persuasion* are both available as Macmillan Readers.

––––––

The Edge of Reason was made into a romantic comedy film released in November 2004. Many of the actors who appeared in *Bridget Jones's Diary* also appear in *The Edge of Reason*. Renée Zellweger, the actress from Texas who plays Bridget, received another Golden Globe Award nomination and also won the People's Choice Award as Favourite Leading Lady of 2005.

However, there are strong differences between the storylines of the book and the film. One main difference is that Daniel Cleaver, Bridget's former boyfriend played by the British actor Hugh Grant, has a major part in the film. But he only makes a short appearance in the book.

Events and References

The Edge of Reason is set in 1997. Helen Fielding has used real-life events as a background for parts of *The Edge of Reason* and she sometimes refers to real people. The main two events featured are:

1 The general election[7], held in Britain on 1 May 1997. In this election, the Labour Party, under the leadership of Tony Blair, beat the Conservative Party (the Tory Party) in a landslide victory – they won the election by a huge majority. Many people saw this victory as a new beginning for Britain.

2 The death of Princess Diana on 31 August 1997. Princess Diana, the divorced[8] wife of Prince Charles and mother of Princes William and Harry, was killed in a car crash in Paris with her friend Dodi Al Fayed. Many people, in Britain and all over the world, were deeply shocked and saddened by her death.

Other references in the story are:

Stone – a unit for measuring weight in the UK containing 14 pounds. 1 stone = 6.35 kilograms. Bridget usually weighs around 9 stone. 9 stone = 57 kilograms.
Calorie – a unit for measuring how much energy you get from food or drink. Doctors in the UK advise that women should not have more than 2000 calories a day and men should not have more than 2500.
Debenhams – a well-known department store in the UK
Valentine's Day – 14 February, the day when it is traditional for people to give cards and presents to the person they love.
Miss Saigon – a popular musical which could be seen in London between 1989 and 1999. It tells the story of an unhappy love affair set in Vietnam, when a Vietnamese bar girl is abandoned[9] by her American soldier lover.

Nat King Cole (1919–1965) – an American musician who came to fame as a jazz pianist and singer, and whose music still remains very popular over forty years after his death. He was the first black American to host a television variety show.

Hampstead Ponds – three large freshwater swimming ponds on Hampstead Heath in North London. One is for men only, one for women only and one for mixed sex bathing.

Temazepam – a drug that is usually prescribed by doctors to treat sleeping problems.

Rudyard Kipling (1865–1936) – an English author and writer best known for his novels and short stories such as *The Jungle Book* and *The Man Who Would Be King*. Kipling was born in India and much of his work is set there. In 1907, he became the first English language writer to win the Nobel Prize. His famous poem *If* is very inspiring and provides a set of rules for life and personal behaviour and development.

Madonna (born in 1958) – an American actress and singer who is sometimes called the 'Queen of Pop'. She won a Golden Globe Award for her role in the 1996 film *Evita*. She married the British film director Guy Ritchie in 2000, although they are now divorced.

DNA – a chemical substance that is found in the cells of all living things and contains genetic information. DNA testing is often used to find out if someone has committed a crime.

The People In This Story

Bridget Jones

Mark Darcy

Jude

Shazzer

Magda

Rebecca

Gary

Bridget's mum

Bridget's dad

Wellington

Una Alconbury

Geoffrey Alconbury

11

1

Happily Ever After

Monday 27 January
Weight 9st 3, boyfriends 1 (great!), calories 1500 (excellent)

7.15 a.m. Hurrah! For four weeks and five days I have been in a relationship with an adult male – my boyfriend, Mark Darcy. I feel marvellous[10]. He is lying beside me now. Ooh. He just moved.

7.30 a.m. I know, I will get up and make him a fantastic breakfast of sausages, eggs and mushrooms.

7.32 a.m. Except I do not have any mushrooms or sausages.

7.33 a.m. Or eggs.

7.34 a.m. Or milk.

7.35 a.m. He still has not woken up. Mmmm. He is lovely. I love looking at him when he is asleep.

7.40 a.m. Maybe I will put … GAAAAAH!

7.50 a.m. That was Mark Darcy sitting up in bed and shouting, 'Bridget, will you stop staring at me when I am asleep. Go and find something to do.'

8.45 a.m. In Coins Café having coffee, a chocolate croissant and a cigarette. It's great to be able to have a cigarette openly. It's very complicated having a man in the house. I have to keep my clothes tidy and not leave them in piles on the floor.

9 a.m. My mother has just walked in, wearing a green jacket with shiny gold buttons.

'Hello, darling,' she said. 'I'm just on my way to Debenhams and I know you always come in here for your breakfast. How's it going with Mark?'

'Lovely,' I said dreamily.

'Oh, and by the way,' said my mother, changing the subject. 'Did I tell you that Una and I are going to Kenya?'

Una Alconbury is my mother's best friend.

'What?' I shouted.

'We're going to Kenya!' she repeated. 'Imagine, darling! To darkest Africa! We want to go on safari and meet the Masai tribesmen[11], then stay in a beach hotel!'

I was shocked. Only a few months ago, my mother went on holiday with Una and met Julio, a Portuguese tour operator. My father got very jealous of Julio. I really don't want Mum to upset Dad again.

11 a.m. Sit Up Britain office. I'm a researcher for a TV news and current affairs[12] programme called *Sit Up Britain*. My boss is the producer, Richard Finch. He's very large and he shouts a lot. When I arrived, he was having a meeting with the other members of the research team.

'Come on, Bridget!' he yelled when he saw me. 'I'm not paying you to be late. I'm paying you to get to work on time and have good ideas.'

11.03 a.m. At my desk. I keep thinking about last night with Mark Darcy.

11.05 a.m. I thought about a book I read recently – *How to Get the Love You Want* – or maybe it was *Keeping the Love You Find?* In this book, it says the man must chase the woman. So I will wait for Mark Darcy to ring me.

11.15 a.m. Richard Finch shouted at me again. He wants me to go to Leicestershire to interview some people who hunt foxes.

11.21 a.m. Telephone.

11.30 a.m. It was my friend Magda. Magda is married to Jeremy and they have three small children. Magda was trying to talk to me, but she kept having to interrupt[13] our conversation to attend to[14] the children.

'Bridget, hi! I was just ringing to ... Do it in the potty[15]! In the potty!' Then there was a terrible sound followed with 'Mummy will smack[16]! Mummy will *smack!*'

'I'm sorry, Magda,' I said. 'But I'm in the middle of work. I've got to leave for Leicestershire in two minutes ...'

'I know you're very important, Bridget,' said Magda. 'I was ringing to say that I've arranged for my builder to come and put up your shelves tomorrow. He's called Gary Wilshaw. Sorry to have bothered you with my boring life. Bye.'

The phone rang again. This time it was my friend Jude. She was crying.

'It's Vile[17] Richard,' she said.

Jude's boyfriend is called Richard. But her friends call him 'Vile Richard' because he treats her so badly.

'I found ... Richard has a self-help book ... book ... called ... called ... *How to Date Young Women: A Guide For Men Over Thirty-Five*. I feel just terrible,' she said. 'Can I see you tonight, Bridge?'

'Um, well, Mark's coming round.'

There was a silence.

'Fine,' she said in a cool voice. 'Have a good time.'

I feel guilty about my friends now that I have a boyfriend. I'm like a traitor[18] in a war. I called Jude back and arranged to see her tomorrow night with our other friend Sharon (Shaz). Now I had better ring Magda and make sure that she doesn't feel boring.

'Thanks, Bridge,' said Magda after we'd talked. 'I'm just feeling depressed since I had the baby. Can you come round tomorrow night?'

'Um, well, I'm supposed to be meeting Jude in Bar 192,' I said.

There was a pause.

'And I suppose I'm too much of a boring Smug Married to come along?' Magda finally said.

My friends and I call married people 'smug' because they always seem so pleased with their lives.

'No, no, come. That would be great!' I said. I knew that Jude would be annoyed that I had invited Magda because she wanted to talk about Vile Richard. But I can't think about that now. I've got to go to Leicestershire. I wonder if I should quickly ring Mark Darcy to tell him where I'm going?

11.35 a.m. Humph[19]. The conversation went like this:

Mark: Yes? Darcy here.

Me: It's Bridget.

Mark: (Pause) Right. Err. Everything OK?

Me: Yes, it was nice last night, wasn't it? I mean, you know, when we …

Mark: Yes. (Pause) I'm actually with the Indonesian Ambassador right now.

Me: Oh. Sorry. I'm just going to Leicestershire.

Mark: Right. Well, ring me when you know what time you're coming back. Bye now.

Hmmm. I don't think I should have called him. It says in one of my books that men really do not like being called when they are busy.

8.30 p.m. Back at my flat. I had a terrible trip to Leicestershire. Everything went wrong. I feel better now. I've tidied my flat, lit the fire and had a bath. I've also washed my hair and put on make-up and sexy black jeans. The jeans are very uncomfortable, but I look nice.

8.35 p.m. Hurrah! It will be a lovely, warm, sexy evening with delicious pasta and firelight. I am a marvellous mixture of a career woman and a girlfriend.

8.40 p.m. Where is he? I'm really fed up …

8.50 p.m. Doorbell. Hurrah! Mark Darcy came in looking really gorgeous[20].

'It's so good to see you,' he whispered into my hair.

I poured him a drink and brought it to him. 'Supper won't be long,' I said. 'I'll just go and check the pasta.' Just then, the phone rang. It was Shaz.

'Hi,' she said. 'How's it going with Mark?'

'He's here,' I whispered, trying to keep my mouth closed so that Mark wouldn't hear.

Mark nodded. 'It's OK,' he said. 'I know I'm here. I don't think we need to keep it a secret from each other.'

'OK. Listen to this,' said Shaz excitedly. 'It's this book called *What Men Want*.' She started reading. '"We are not saying that all men cheat[21]. But all men do think about cheating."'

'Actually, Shaz, I'm just cooking pasta,' I said.

'"If you have a beautiful sister,"' Shaz went on, '"or friend, be sure that your boyfriend is HAVING THOUGHTS ABOUT SEX WITH HER."'

'Shaz, can we talk about this tomorrow?'

I put the phone down. I had just put the pasta in a bowl when it rang again. This time it was Jude. Mark did not look very pleased. But Jude and Shaz are my friends. They'd been kind to me for years before I met Mark. So I have to talk to them when they call.

Jude was depressed because she had read an article about single girls over thirty. According to the article, all that girls over thirty want is to get married and have babies. But I told Jude that I thought this was rubbish and as we chatted[22], she became more cheerful. Then I put the phone down and went back to join Mark at the table.

Unfortunately the pasta did not look very good. There was a lot of water in it. So we ordered pizzas and ate them in front of the fire.

Mark started talking to me about his day at work. Then the phone rang again.

'Don't answer it,' said Mark.

It was Jude again. 'Bridget, I think I've done the wrong thing. I called Stacey, this guy at work, and he hasn't called me back.'

I talked to Jude for some time. I told her that Stacey would ring tomorrow. When I put the phone down, Mark was watching football. I stared at him.

'Do you want to have sex with Shazzer?' I asked.

'I'm sorry?'

'Do you want to sleep with Shazzer and Jude?'

'Do you mean separately?' he asked. 'Or both at the same time?'

'But have you ever thought about it?' I asked.

'Well,' said Mark, laughing. 'They are very attractive girls.'

Just as we'd cleared away the plates, the phone rang again.

'Leave it,' said Mark. 'Please.'

The answer phone was on. We heard a man's voice.

'Ah, hi. Giles Benwick here. I'm a friend of Mark's. I don't suppose he's there, is he? It's just ...' Suddenly his voice broke. 'My wife's just told me she wants a separation and ...'

Mark grabbed the phone. There was an expression of panic[23] on his face. 'Giles, wait ... um ... ah ... Giles, I think Bridget should talk to you.'

I did not know Giles, but I think I gave him good advice. I managed to calm him and recommended some self-help books to him. Afterwards I had a lovely time with Mark. I felt very safe and warm with him.

2

Jellyfish[24] Alert

Tuesday 28 January

Weight 9st 2, cigarettes smoked in front of Mark 0 (very good), cigarettes smoked in secret 7

8 a.m. At my flat. Mark has gone back to his flat to change before work. I'm just going to have a little cigarette and ... Gaaah! Doorbell.

8.30 a.m. It was Magda's builder, Gary. I forgot he was coming round.

'Would you like some tea or coffee?' I asked.

'Yeah. Cup of tea,' he replied. 'With four teaspoons of sugar.'

'Right,' I said. 'Right.' I started making the tea while Gary sat down at the kitchen table. Then I realized I didn't have any milk or sugar.

'I'll just pop round to the shop,' I said.

When I came back, Gary was still sitting at the kitchen table. He started telling me a long, complicated story about fishing. At last I managed to interrupt him.

'Right. Shall I show you what I want you to do?' I said. Then I felt guilty because Gary would think I was not interested in him as a person, only as a workman.

8 p.m. I got home to find Gary the Builder still there. There were dirty plates and magazines about fishing everywhere.

'What do you think?' said Gary proudly, pointing towards the shelves.

'They're great!' I said quickly, and I swallowed[25] hard at the same time. 'But err ... could you put the shelf supports in line with each other?'

'But err … could you put the shelf supports
in line with each other?'

The supports were put in different places on each level, making the whole thing look very untidy.

'Yeah, well, you see, if I drill[26] holes in the wall here, all your electricity will go off,' Gary began. Then the phone rang. It was Mark. I could hear the noise of traffic in the background.

'Have you got someone there?' asked Mark.

'No,' I replied. 'It's just the …' I was about to say 'builder' but I did not want to hurt Gary's feelings, so I changed it to 'Gary – a friend of Magda's.'

'I'm in the car. Do you want to come out for supper tonight with Giles?' asked Mark.

'I've said I'll see the girls.'

'Oh. I suppose you'll all be talking about me,' he said. 'I met your friend Rebecca the other day. She seemed very nice.'

'I didn't know you knew Rebecca,' I said, breathing very quickly.

Rebecca is not really a friend, except that she's always coming to Bar 192 with me and Jude and Shaz. Rebecca is a 'jellyfisher'. A jellyfish looks harmless but it can sting[27] you. It's the same with Rebecca. You can have a conversation with her that seems nice and friendly, then you suddenly feel as if you've been stung. For example, if you're talking about jeans, she'll say, 'Yes, well, if you've got fat legs, then you'll look best in something really well cut.'

'Bridge, are you still there?' asked Mark.

'Where did you see Rebecca?' I said in a high voice.

'She was at a drinks party last night and introduced herself,' Mark explained.

'Last night?'

'Yes,' he said. 'I dropped in[28] on my way over to your flat.'

'What did you talk about?' I asked.

'Oh, you know. She asked about my work and said nice things about you,' Mark said. 'She said you were a free spirit[29]…'

Free spirit? That's Rebecca's way of saying, 'Bridget sleeps with lots of men and drinks too much.'

Gary was still talking about the electrical problem.

'Well, have a good time,' said Mark. 'I'll call you later.'

After I put down the phone, I couldn't think properly.

'He's interested in someone else, is he?' said Gary.

I looked at him angrily. 'What about these shelves …?'

'Well,' he replied. 'If you want them to be straight, I'll have to change all your electric leads and …'

'The shelves are fine,' I said. 'Just lovely.'

I've just paid Gary a lot of money to get him out of the flat. Oh God, I am so late. The telephone is ringing again.

9.05 p.m. It was Dad.

'I just called to see how you were.' He sounded very strange.

'I'm fine,' I said. 'How are you? How's Mum?'

'Ah. Well, she's, she's ah …' There was a long, painful pause. Then he said, 'She's going to Kenya. With Una.'

'Oh. Did she ask you to go too?' I asked.

'Ah. Well. You see, no. Bridget, I'm so upset. Remember what happened last time she went on holiday with Una? She met that awful Portuguese man, Julio. Now she'll probably get herself a Kenyan boyfriend.'

I felt shocked. I did not know what advice to give Dad. In the end, I told him to be calm and discuss things with Mum in the morning.

Wednesday 29 January
Weight 9st 5, cigarettes 1 (very good), jobs 1, flats 1, boyfriends 1

5.15 a.m. I keep remembering last night.

I rushed to Bar 192. Jude kept talking about a depressing book she had read about women over thirty.

Just then Magda arrived. I poured her a glass of wine.

'Hi, Magda,' said Jude. 'When are you going to have your baby?'

'I had my baby five weeks ago,' replied Magda. Then she turned and whispered, 'Do I look fat?' to me as if Jude and Shazzer were her enemies.

'No,' I said. 'You look great.'

'Do I?' said Magda. 'Thank you, Bridget. How are things with Mark?'

'Lovely,' I said happily. 'He makes me feel so ...' I saw Jude and Shazzer glance[30] at each other. I realized I probably sounded smug because I was in a relationship with a lovely man. 'The only problem is ... he called me tonight and said he'd met Rebecca.'

'WHATTTTT?' shouted Sharon. 'Where?'

'At a party last night,' I said.

'What was he doing at a party last night?' yelled Jude. 'Without you?'

Shaz, Jude and I discussed Mark's phone call. Why hadn't Mark told me about the party or Rebecca until *twenty-four hours* later?

Suddenly Jude said, 'ALERT, ALERT, JELLYFISH ALERT.'

We looked out of the window and saw Rebecca getting out of a car across the street. A few minutes later, she walked into the bar, swinging her long blonde hair so that it fell over her face like a shiny curtain.

'How are things going with Mark?' she asked me as she sat down. 'You must be really pleased to have a boyfriend at last. Is he taking you to the Law Society Dinner on Friday?'

Mark hadn't said anything to me about the Law Society Dinner.

'Oh, sorry, have I said something wrong?' asked Rebecca. 'I'm sure he's just forgotten to ask you.'

8.30 a.m. Why hasn't Mark Darcy rung me?

A few minutes later, she walked into the bar,
swinging her long blonde hair …

Thursday 30 January

9 a.m. Coins Café. Having coffee. Hurrah! Everything is lovely. Mark just rang! And he's asked me to come to the Law Society Dinner tomorrow.

9.05 a.m. It's a bit scary though. It's a 'black tie' dinner – which means it's very formal.

9.15 a.m. It's very important to make a good impression on Mark's friends at the dinner. I am going to be marvellous: elegant[31] and beautifully dressed.

6 p.m. Just leaving the office. I'm going shopping with Magda to buy some special underwear. She's going to lend me a very elegant, long dark-blue dress. She says I need to wear underwear that will control my figure and make me look slim.

9 p.m. Back home. Magda made me buy a very scary, tight corset[32] to wear under my dress. It kept unrolling itself down my body.

'What if Mark sees me or feels me in this?' I said worriedly.

'You're going to a formal dinner, Bridget,' Magda replied. 'Mark will be busy trying to make a good impression on his colleagues. He'll be concentrating on that – not on trying to touch you.'

3

The Law Society Dinner

Friday 31 January
Weight 9st 4, cigarettes 12, calories 4284

9.30 a.m. I am very excited about the Law Society Dinner. I have been practising wearing my dress and it looks excellent.

Midnight. When I arrived at the Guildhall, where the dinner was being held, Mark was walking up and down outside. When he saw me, he looked really shocked, then he laughed.

'Sorry I'm late,' I said breathlessly.

'You're not,' he said. He looked at me again strangely.

We went inside.

'I think you should go to the ladies' room and look at your face,' Mark whispered in my ear.

When I looked in the mirror, I had a shock. I had put my make-up on in the taxi, but in the darkness I had put dark grey eye shadow[33] all over my cheeks instead of blusher[34].

I cleaned my face and came out of the ladies' room to see Mark talking to Rebecca.

'Oh, Bridget,' said Rebecca, laughing into Mark's face. 'How are you, lovely girl?' She kissed me. 'Are you feeling nervous?'

'Nervous?' said Mark. 'Why would she be nervous?'

For a moment, Rebecca looked annoyed. Then she said, 'Ahhh, isn't that sweet? I'm so happy for you.'

'She always seems extremely nice and intelligent,' said Mark after Rebecca had left us.

Always? I was thinking. *Always??* I thought he'd only met her twice. He put his arm round me but it almost touched my corset so I jumped away.

We went through to the dining room. It looked very elegant. There was a lot of dark wood, candlelight and shining glass, and there were round tables. A group of very confident lawyers in their thirties was sitting at our table. They were laughing loudly at each others' jokes.

I sat quietly and ate my food. Then they started talking about politics. Suddenly Mark said, 'If I'm going to vote[35] Tory again, I need to know that my views are being properly represented in Parliament.'

I stared at him in horror. I knew there were differences between Mark and me. But I had never suspected he voted Tory. Suddenly I felt that I did not know Mark Darcy at all.

'Are you all right?' whispered Mark. 'You're … *shaking*. What is it?'

I told him.

'So I vote Tory. What's wrong with that?' he said, staring at me in surprise. 'What do you vote?'

'Labour, of course. Everybody votes Labour. The Tories are rubbish.'

'Rubbish?' said Mark. 'The economy's better now than it's been in seven years.'

'Look,' I said. 'Labour stands for being left-wing[36].' For some reason Mark seemed to find this very funny. 'They stand for the principles[37] of sharing, kindness, single mothers and Nelson Mandela,' I went on. 'That's much better than loud, bossy men having affairs[38] and staying in expensive hotels.'

There was a huge silence round the table.

'Well,' said Mark, laughing. 'We can't argue with that.'

Later there were speeches. They were very long and boring. As soon as they were over, Mark whispered, 'Let's get out of here, shall we?'

We said our goodbyes and set off across the room.

'Err … Bridget,' he said. 'I don't want to worry you. But there's something strange round your waist.'

26

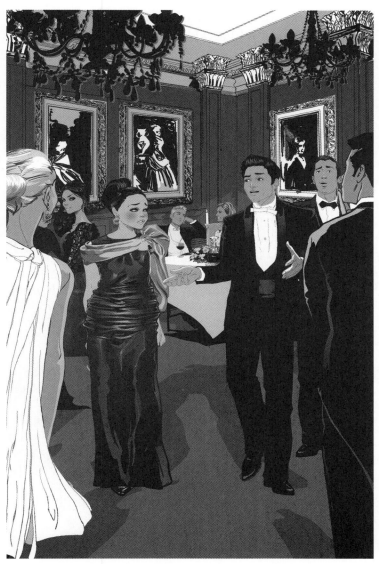

'There's something strange round your waist.'

I looked down. The scary corset had unrolled itself and was sat round my waist like a huge tyre. I rushed to the ladies' room and took off the dress and the scary corset, then put everything on again. When I walked back into the hall, Mark was talking to Rebecca. She whispered something in his ear, then laughed.

'Bridget!' said Rebecca, pretending to be pleased to see me.

'We must go,' said Mark. 'It was nice to see you again, Rebecca.'

Rebecca went back into the dining room. I couldn't think what to say as Mark and I walked to the car.

As we were driving, Mark said, 'Oh, Rebecca asked if we wanted to go round for dinner sometime.'

I couldn't believe this. I've known Rebecca for four years and she has never asked me round for dinner.

'She looked nice, didn't she?' said Mark. 'Nice dress.'

Mark was driving towards my house. Suddenly I felt angry. Why didn't he want to take me to *his* house? It was probably full of messages from Rebecca.

'Where are we going?' I said suddenly.

'Your flat. Why?' he said in surprise.

'Exactly. Why?' I asked angrily. 'We've been going out for five weeks. And we've never once stayed at your house. Why?'

Mark went completely silent. Then he turned the car around and drove towards Holland Park Avenue, the area of London where he lived.

When we got to his house, it was awful. We walked up the steps to the front door in silence. He opened the door and put the lights on in the kitchen. It was very modern with a lot of stainless steel[39].

'Would you like a glass of wine?' asked Mark.

'Yes, please, thank you,' I said.

Mark started opening doors. He was looking for the fridge. But he didn't seem to know where it was. At last he found it and poured some wine. He stood in front of me, looking really miserable.

'Look, Bridget, I ...'

I got off the stool to put my arms round him. Immediately he put his hands on my waist. I pulled away. I didn't want him to find out about the corset.

'What's the matter?' asked Mark.

'Nothing,' I said. 'I think I'd just like to go home.'

'I don't understand,' said Mark. 'First, you want to come back to my house, and then you want to leave.' He sounded upset.

'I'm sorry, Mark,' I said. 'I'm just tired.'

I went straight home and took off the corset. Then I started worrying about Mark. I'm going to call him first thing tomorrow morning and tell him I'm sorry.

Saturday 1 February

9 a.m. Gaah! Gaah! Telephone. Hurrah!

9.30 a.m. It was my mother.

'Daddy and I thought you and Mark might like to come to lunch tomorrow,' she said.

'Can I ring you back later, Mum?' I said quickly. I had to get off the phone so Mark could call.

The phone rang again. This time it was Shazzer. I started to tell her about my evening with Mark.

'Listen, Bridget,' she said. 'Get out of the relationship with Mark. Get out before it's too late. You've had the warning sign. He votes Tory.'

Then Jude rang. I told her about Mark voting Tory.

When I had finished, Jude said, 'I've been reading a book called *Women Who Love Too Much*. Just detach[40] yourself,

29

Bridget. Remove yourself quietly from the relationship. Don't call him.'

11.15 a.m. I've arranged to meet Jude and Shazzer in Bar 192 for lunch. I am going to be completely detached.

11.18 a.m. I can't believe he still hasn't called me.

Noon. Mark rang.

'How are you?' he said. He sounded very tired.

'I'm fine,' I said, trying to be detached.

'Shall I pick you up and we can go for lunch?'

'Um, I'm having lunch with the girls,' I said in a very detached way. 'Why didn't you call before?'

'Every time I tried to call, your number was busy.'

I've arranged to meet him for dinner.

Sunday 2 February

Weight 9st 2, cigarettes 3 (very good) calories 2100, boyfriends 1 again (hurrah!)

10 p.m. At my flat. At dinner last night Mark said, 'Bridge? Last night I felt things weren't right between us.'

I felt a terrible pain. Was Mark going to end our relationship?

'Why?' I whispered.

'Well, every time I tried to touch you, you moved away.'

I felt a huge sense of relief. I explained to him about the scary corset, and he started to laugh.

Next morning at my flat, Mark was looking at my shelves.

'Those shelf supports aren't level,' he said. Then he said, 'What are all these books?' He got up and looked at them. 'Are you trying to cover yourself both ways? *Happy to Be Single* with *How to Find your Perfect Partner in Thirty Days?*'

'They're my self-help books,' I said.

Mark was smiling at me. 'Why do you buy this stuff?'

Just then the phone rang. It was my mum.

'I thought you and Mark were coming to lunch today,' she said.

'But, Mum …' Then my dad came on the phone.

'Don't worry, my dear. I'm sure you didn't tell her you were coming. I'll try to calm her down.'

Mum grabbed the phone. 'Una and I are definitely going to Kenya next Saturday. Just for ten days. Africa! Imagine!'

That evening, Mark and I went round to his house and lit candles in the bedroom. Hurrah! I love Mark Darcy. Sometimes he seems scary but underneath he is very kind and sweet. That's good, I think.

Especially as Valentine's Day is in twelve days' time.

4

Valentine's Day

Monday 3 February
Weight 9st (very good), cigarettes 12, number of days to Valentine's Day 11

8.45 a.m. Telephone! It was Mark. He is going to New York tomorrow for two weeks.

I managed to say, 'Oh, that's nice.' But after I had put the phone down, I yelled, 'But it's Valentine's Day a week on[41] Friday, it's Valentine's Day. Baaaaaaah!'

Tuesday 4 February

8 a.m. In café having coffee and chocolate croissant. I am not thinking negative thoughts about Mark going away. It will give me a chance to do other things.

Plan for when Mark is away
1 Go to the gym every day.
2 Have lots of lovely evenings with Shazzer and Jude.
3 Continue to sort out my flat.
4 Spend time with Dad when Mum is away.
5 Really work hard at work to improve my position.
6 Lose weight, of course.

Thursday 13 February
Weight 9st 3, cigarettes 19, gym visits 0, early Valentine's gifts 0

I am very fed up. It's Valentine's Day tomorrow and Mark has not even mentioned it.

Goals achieved in Mark's absence
Number of gym visits 0
Evenings spent with Jude and Shazzer 6
Minutes spent with Dad 0
Pounds lost 0
Pounds gained 3

Friday 14 February

Weight 9st 4, gym visits 0, flowers 0, Valentine's gifts 0, difference between Valentine's Day and any other day 0

8 a.m. I don't care about Valentine's Day. It's just not important.

8.20 a.m. I will just go downstairs and see if the post has come.

8.22 a.m. The post has not come.

8.27 a.m. The post has still not come.

8.30 a.m. The post has come! Hurrah!

8.35 a.m. It was a letter from my bank. Nothing from Mark, nothing, nothing, nothing, nothing, nothing, nothing. Nothing.

8.40 a.m. I cannot believe I am spending Valentine's Day alone again. I feel very sad. Mark just doesn't care.

10 p.m. I cannot believe what has happened. At half past eleven, a young man came into the office carrying an enormous bunch of red roses and brought them to my desk.

Richard Finch just stared.

There was a card with the roses. I opened it and this is what it said:

*Happy Valentine's Day! Be at Heathrow Airport, Terminal
1, tomorrow to pick up a ticket from British Airways for a
magical mystery mini-break. I will meet you at the other
end. (Try to borrow a ski suit and some sensible shoes.)*

Mark is taking me on a Valentine's ski surprise. Hurrah! It will
be very romantic. Jude has lent me a black ski suit. I've only
been skiing once. I went when I was at school. Never mind.
I'm sure it will be easy.

Saturday 15 February

2.30 p.m. Mountain café. I hadn't realized what a dangerous
sport skiing is. People have terrible accidents. I told Mark Darcy,
who is very good at skiing, that skiing is very dangerous.

Mark listened quietly and thoughtfully. Then he said, 'But
this is the beginners' slope, Bridget. It's almost flat. And skiing
is like everything else in life. It's all about confidence.'

5 p.m. Mark helped me practise skiing. Then we went back to
the mountain café for a rest. Suddenly Mark was greeted by a
group of people who looked like lawyers and bankers. Among
them was a tall, thin, blonde girl in a white ski suit. She was
laughing loudly. It was Rebecca.

'Bridget!' she said, kissing me. 'How fantastic to see you!
What a coincidence[42]!'

I looked at Mark, who looked confused.

'Um, it's not really a coincidence, is it?' he said. 'You
suggested that I should bring Bridget here. I didn't know you
were all going to be here too.'

Rebecca smiled.

'I think I'll just go and do some more practice,' I whispered
to Mark.

I went up on the lift to the top of the beginners' slope but
something didn't feel right. It was bumpy and uncomfortable.

Suddenly I saw all Mark's friends shouting and waving from the café balcony. Then Mark started to run towards me from the direction of the café.

'Bridget,' he yelled. 'You've forgotten to put your skis on!'

I went back to the café and had a delicious hot chocolate. While I was drinking it, Mark went skiing with Rebecca. I watched them coming down the mountain. They looked like a perfect couple in a skiing brochure.

'Oh, it's so exciting,' said Rebecca, laughing into Mark's face. 'Listen, do you want to have supper with us tonight?'

'No,' said Mark quickly. 'I'm taking Bridget for a Valentine's dinner.'

For a moment Rebecca looked annoyed. Then she said, 'OK, have fun.' She skied off towards the town.

'When did you see her?' I asked. 'When did she suggest coming here?'

'She was in New York,' said Mark.

I dropped one of my ski poles. Mark laughed and gave me a big hug.

'Don't worry,' he said. 'She was there with a crowd. I had one ten-minute conversation with her. I said I wanted to do something nice to make up for[43] missing Valentine's Day and she suggested coming here.'

I made a small noise.

'Bridget,' he said. 'I love you.'

Sunday 16 February

Weight – do not care, number of times I have replayed wonderful L-word in my head – so many that I have lost count

I am so happy. I do not feel angry about Rebecca. Mark and I had a lovely fun dinner with lots of laughing and said how much we'd missed each other.

'Bridget,' he yelled. 'You've forgotten to put your skis on!'

Monday 17 February

Weight 9st 6, cigarettes 12, embarrassing acts by my mother 1

The mini-break was fantastic, apart from Rebecca. But I had a shock at Heathrow Airport this morning. We were standing in the arrivals hall looking for the taxi sign when a voice said: 'Darling! You shouldn't have come to meet me. Geoffrey and Daddy are waiting for us outside. Come and meet Wellington!'

It was my mother. Her skin was tanned[44] bright orange and she was wearing a large African outfit in orange material.

'I know you're going to think he's a Masai but he's a Kikuyu[45]! Imagine!'

I looked to where Una Alconbury, also orange and dressed in a strange African outfit, was standing in a shop. She was looking up into the face of an enormous black youth. He was dressed in a bright blue cloak[46].

'*Hakuna Matata*,' said my mother. 'Don't worry, be happy. Swahili. Isn't it great? Una and I have had a wonderful time and Wellington's come back to stay! Hello, Mark.'

'Shut up, Mother, shut up,' I whispered out of the corner of my mouth. 'You can't have an African tribesman to stay.'

'Wellington is not a tribesman,' said my mother. 'Well, he does live in a hut. But he wants to do worldwide travel.'

I wish I had a normal mum like other people, with grey hair, who would cook lovely meals.

Tuesday 18 February

Weight 9st 6, cigarettes 13, fantasies about Mark being in love with Rebecca 42

7 p.m. I got back from work in a rush. Shaz has decided that she likes football, so Jude and I are going round to her house to watch a football match.

There was a message on my answer phone from Mark. He said he was going out to a business dinner that evening. He would ring me at Shaz's later to find out about the football.

Then he paused and said, 'Oh and, err, Rebecca has invited us to her parents' house in Gloucestershire for a house party next weekend. What do you think?'

I think I would rather sit in a little hole in Mum and Dad's garden all weekend than go to Rebecca's house party and watch her flirting with Mark.

The telephone rang. It was Magda.

'Oh, Bridget! Hi! How was the skiing?'

'It was great but ...' I told her the whole story about Rebecca, New York and the house party. 'I don't know if I should go or not.'

'Of course, you've got to go, Bridge,' said Magda. 'Just go along, be gorgeous and keep an eye on Rebecca.'

Midnight. Back at flat. Shaz, Jude and I watched the football match. But I couldn't concentrate because I was thinking about Rebecca's invitation.

'Are you all right, Bridge?' asked Jude. 'You seem a bit depressed.'

'Rebecca rang Mark and asked us to go on a mini-break at her parents' house next weekend,' I explained.

'WHAT?' shouted Jude and Shaz together.

'We've known Rebecca for four years,' said Shaz. 'Has she ever once, in all that time, invited you, me or Jude on one of her house-party weekends?'

'No,' I said, shaking my head.

'But if you don't go,' said Jude, 'what happens if Rebecca gets hold of Mark?'

The phone rang. It was Mark.

'What happened in the football?' he asked excitedly.

'Um ...' I said, looking at Jude and Shazzer.

'You did watch it, didn't you?' asked Mark.

'Yes, we did. But we were … talking,' I finished weakly.

'Oh God.' There was a long silence. 'Listen, do you want to go to Rebecca's?'

I looked from Jude to Shaz wildly.

'Yes,' I said.

'Oh great,' Mark said. 'It'll be fun, I think. She said to bring a swimsuit.'

5

Problems

Gloucestershire. Rebecca's parents' place is huge. It has stables for horses, outbuildings and a pool. As we arrived, we saw Rebecca playing with a dog in the garden. The sun was shining on her hair. She looked like a girl in an advertisement.

'Come and have a drink,' she said, leading Mark away.

My mobile rang. It was my mother.

'Oh, hello, darling, guess what? We're all going to *Miss Saigon* next Friday! Una and Geoffrey and Daddy and I and Wellington. And we've got tickets for you and Mark!'

By the time I got into the house, Mark and Rebecca had disappeared.

4 p.m. I just got back from a walk round the garden. Rebecca was walking in front with Mark. I started walking with Rebecca's teenage nephew. Everyone called him 'Johnny's boy.' He offered me a cigarette.

'I'd better not,' I said, nodding in Mark's direction.

'Is he your boyfriend or your father?' said Johnny's boy.

We went off the path towards a small lake. It was very nice smoking and laughing together. Then we had to run to catch up with the others. When we found them, Mark put his arms round me.

'What have you been doing?' he asked. 'Smoking like a naughty schoolgirl?'

'I haven't had a cigarette for five years,' laughed Rebecca.

Midnight. Rebecca put me beside Johnny's boy at dinner. Then she put herself next to Mark. They looked perfect together.

When dinner was over, she said, 'Shall we change into our swimwear now?' She came back a few minutes later in a beautifully cut swimsuit.

'Mark,' she said. 'Would you help me take the cover off the pool?'

Mark looked from her to me worriedly.

'Of course. Yes,' he said uncomfortably, and he disappeared after her.

'Are you going to swim?' asked Johnny's boy.

'No,' I replied. 'It's eleven o'clock at night and I've had a huge dinner.'

I noticed that all the other guests were leaving the room.

'Shall we go and have coffee?' I said, getting up.

Suddenly Johnny's boy leaned forwards and started trying to kiss me. The door burst open. It was Mark and Rebecca.

'Oops! Sorry!' said Rebecca, and she shut the door.

'What do you think you're doing?' I said to Johnny's boy, horrified.

'But … Rebecca said you told her you really fancied me, and … and … she said you and Mark were breaking up.'

I grabbed the table for support. 'Who told her that?'

'She said,' – he looked really embarrassed – 'she said Mark did.'

Sunday 23 February
Weight 12st 4 (probably), cigarettes 100 000 (it feels like), calories 3275, positive thoughts 0

When I woke up this morning, Mark was already dressed.

'I can explain what happened,' I said. 'Rebecca told her nephew that I fancied him and … and that you told her we were … breaking up.'

Mark sat down and started rubbing his forehead.

'Did you?' I whispered. 'Did you say that to Rebecca?'

'No,' he said after a few seconds. 'I didn't say that. But ... maybe we ...'

There was a knock at the door. It was Rebecca, looking beautiful in a pink jumper.

'It's breakfast time,' she said.

Later Mark and I drove home in silence.

'Don't do this!' I wanted to yell when we stopped outside my flat. 'She's trying to steal you. I didn't kiss that boy. I love you.'

But instead, all I said was, 'Well, bye then.'

'Bye,' he said, not looking at me.

I watched him turn the car around really fast and drive off.

Monday 24 February
Weight 15st, cigarettes 200 000, calories 8477

3 a.m. As soon as Mark had driven off yesterday, I called Shaz and Jude. They came round within fifteen minutes with pizza, ice cream and chocolates.

'Do you think I should call him?' I asked.

'No!' yelled Shaz.

'Are you crazy?' said Jude.

'But what if ...?' I said.

'You'd better unplug the phone, Shaz,' said Jude. 'Or she'll spend all night waiting for him to ring.'

Shaz pulled the phone out of the wall.

We ate the food and talked. We had a very good time. But now I am really missing Mark.

7 p.m. Wild joy! I got home to find the answer phone light flashing.

'Bridget, hi, it's Mark. I don't know where you were last night, but I'm just calling to see how you are. I'll try you again later.'

7.13 p.m. He hasn't rung. I don't know what to do now. I'd better ring Shaz.

In addition to my other problems, there's something wrong with my hair.

7.30 p.m. I played Mark's message over the phone to Shaz and said, 'Should I call him back?'

'No!' said Shaz.

8.50 p.m. I was just about to ring Mark and tell him how much I liked him, but fortunately Jude rang before I could pick up the phone.

'Should I ring him tomorrow maybe?' I asked.

'No!' she said.

11 p.m. Mark hasn't rung. I am so confused.

Tuesday 25 February

8 p.m. Magda just called. I told her about the weekend.

'So what does Mark say about it?' she asked.

'I haven't spoken to him.'

'But, Bridget, he hasn't ended the relationship with you. He just got in a bad mood because he thought you were kissing someone. You should call him.'

8.45 p.m. Maybe Magda is right. I am going to call him.

9.10 p.m. Mark Darcy answered by saying 'Yessss?' impatiently down the phone. There was a lot of noise in the background.

'It's me, Bridget,' I whispered.

'Bridget! You haven't called me for two days and now you ring me in the middle of an important football match. Look, I'll call you back later.'

9.35 p.m. Oh goody – telephone. Mark Darcy!

It was Jude. 'What?' she said. 'He didn't talk to you because he was in the middle of a *football match?*'

Jude said if Mark really cared about me, football would not have been important. I called Shaz and told her what had happened. She completely agreed with Jude.

'Men only like football because they're lazy,' Shaz said.

'You're right,' I said. 'So are you coming round to Jude's?'

'Err, no …' Shaz said.

'Why not?' I asked.

'I'm watching the match with Simon,' she said.

Simon? Shazzer and *Simon?* But Simon is just one of our friends.

'But I thought you just said …?'

'That's different,' she replied. 'I like football because it's a very interesting game.'

Hmmm. I was just leaving the flat when my mother rang.

'Remember we've bought the tickets for *Miss Saigon* on Friday,' she said. I had forgotten all about *Miss Saigon*.

'I don't think Mark can come,' I said. 'He's working.'

'Working!' said my mother. 'What's he doing working on a Friday night?'

'Mum, I've really got to go. I'm going round to Jude's and I'm late,' I said.

When I got home from Jude's, Mark rang.

'Sorry about earlier,' he said. 'I'm really depressed about it, aren't you?'

'I know,' I said lovingly. 'I feel exactly the same.'

'I just keep thinking: why?'

'Exactly!' I said, feeling a great rush of love.

'If he hadn't been sent off, we would never have lost the match.'

I gave a cry. Mark had been talking about the *football match*, not our relationship.

'Shall I come round tomorrow?' he said. 'No, wait, I'm playing football. Thursday?'

'Err ... yes,' I said.

'Great, see you about eight o'clock.'

Wednesday 26 February
Weight 9st 4, cigarettes 3 (very good), calories 3845 (poor)

7.30 p.m. Doorbell. It can't be Mark. He definitely said tomorrow!

'Who is it?' I asked through the entry phone.

'It's Gary,' said a voice.

'Oh hi, hi.' I didn't have any idea who Gary was. 'How are you?' I said.

'Cold,' he replied. 'Are you going to let me in?'

I suddenly remembered. Gary was the builder who came to put up my shelves. 'Oh, *Gary*,' I said. 'Come on up!'

Gary came in wearing jeans which were covered with paint.

'Hi,' he said, sitting down at the kitchen table as if he were my husband.

'Now, Gary,' I said. 'I'm in a bit of a hurry.'

Gary said nothing and started rolling a cigarette. Then he started talking about building projects. He stood up and went through to the bedroom. I stood nervously in the bedroom doorway, while he opened the window and looked out.

'You've got room for an extension out here,' he said. 'You could have a second bedroom with a little roof terrace on top.'

Roof terrace? Second bedroom? I could make it into an office and work at home.

'How much would it cost?' I asked.

'I'll think about it and call you,' Gary replied.

He picked up his coat and cigarettes, opened his bag and laid a magazine down on the table. As he reached the door, he looked at me. 'Page seventy-one,' he said.

I picked up the magazine, thinking it was going to be about building projects. But it was a magazine about fishing. On page seventy-one there was a picture of Gary, smiling proudly and holding up a huge grey fish.

Thursday 27 February
Weight 9st 3, cigarettes 17, calories 625

Midnight. This has been a terrible evening. Mark had just come in the door when the phone rang.

'Hi, doll, it's Gary here.' He was leaving a message on my answer phone, which meant that Mark could hear every word. Oh God. How dare[47] he speak to me in such a familiar[48] way?

'Right,' Gary went on. 'What we were talking about in the bedroom – I've got some ideas so give me a ring and I'll come round.'

Mark looked down at the floor.

'OK,' he said. 'Do you want to explain?'

'It's the builder,' I said. 'Magda's builder, Gary. The one that put the shelves up. He wants to build an extension.'

'I see,' he said.

Just then the fax machine started making a noise. A fax was coming through. Mark pulled it out and read it. It was from Jude. There was a photograph of a handsome male model taken from a magazine and the words, 'Who needs Mark Darcy when you can have one of these?' underneath.

Friday 28 February

Weight 9st 2 (the only good thing that has happened)

Midnight. I went to see *Miss Saigon* with Mum and Dad, Una and Geoffrey Alconbury and Wellington. Wellington was wearing one of Dad's suits.

'So!' said Una. 'Where's Mark?'

'He's working this evening,' I said, as Dad and Uncle Geoffrey came over to us.

'That's what your last boyfriend said, didn't he?' shouted Geoffrey. 'It's always the same with my little Bridget. All her boyfriends run away.'

'Do you have older women who can't get married in your tribe, Wellington?' asked Una.

'I am not an older woman,' I said.

'When she is older, with or without a husband, a woman has the respect of the tribe,' said Wellington, smiling at me.

When the show was over, we drove to my flat in Geoffrey and Una's car.

Suddenly Una said, 'Isn't that Mark?'

'Where?' asked Mum.

'Over there,' said Una. I looked over and saw Mark, dressed in a dark blue overcoat, getting out of a taxi. Then I saw a figure getting out of the back. She was tall and slim, with long blonde hair, and she was laughing up into Mark's face. It was Rebecca.

Mum and Una immediately began talking loudly. 'Well, I think it's absolutely disgusting! With another woman on a Friday night when he said he was working!'

Wellington and I were silent. Then Wellington took my hand and held it, very still and strong, without saying a word.

Then I saw a figure getting out of the back.

6

The Hole in the Wall

Saturday 1 March

10 p.m. My flat. Very black day. Jude, Shaz and I went out shopping, then came back here to get ready for a party. There was a message on my answer phone from Mark which I played to them.

'Hi, Bridget. You don't seem to be returning my calls,' he said. 'I really think, whatever, I … I'm really … We – at least I feel – I owe it to you to be friends. Oh God, give me a ring soon. If you want to.'

'He seems to have forgotten he's run off with Rebecca,' said Jude. 'You've really got to detach now, Bridget.'

At that moment the phone rang.

'Hi.' It was Mark. I felt a great wave of love in my heart. 'Did you get your message? I mean *my* message?' he asked.

'Yes,' I said. 'But I got it just after I saw you getting out of a taxi with Rebecca, who has been trying to steal you for a month. So I wasn't in a very good mood.'

'But it wasn't my fault,' he replied. 'I can explain.'

'Yes – to say you owe it to me to be my friend,' I said in a high voice. 'But I don't need a friend like you. I already have the best, most loyal[49], supportive friends in the world.'

'All right,' said Mark. 'If you don't want me to explain, I won't trouble you with phone calls. Goodbye, Bridget.'

I put down the phone and looked round at my friends. Shaz was lying on the carpet, waving a cigarette, and Jude was drinking out of a bottle of wine. Suddenly I had an awful feeling I had made a terrible mistake.

Sunday 2 March

10.30 a.m. I've just woken up. I got home really late from the party last night. Oooh, telephone.

11.15 a.m. It was my mother.
'Bridget, why are you still at home? You're supposed to be coming to lunch today.'

Monday 3 March
Weight 9st 5 (after Sunday lunch at my parents' yesterday), cigarettes 17

8 a.m. When I arrived at my parents' house yesterday, Mum and Una were busy in the kitchen preparing lunch. Dad and Geoffrey Alconbury were talking. Wellington was out in the garden practising football.

'He doesn't like formal lunches,' said Mum. 'Now, come on, Bridget, help me. They're going to be here in a moment.'

'Who?' I asked suspiciously[50].

'The Darcys.'

'The Darcys? Mark's parents? Now? Why?'

Just then the doorbell rang. Mum and Una rushed off.

I followed Dad into the lounge. Mark's mum and dad were standing in a circle with Una and Geoffrey. They were each holding a drink.

'So how's your son?' asked Una.

'My son! Well, he's getting married,' said Mark's father. I started to feel faint[51]. Getting married?

'I think Una was asking about Mark, not Peter, darling,' said Mark's mum, looking at me in an understanding way. 'Peter is our other son out in Hong Kong. He's getting married in June.'

We went through to the dining room and had lunch. Mum started talking brightly about *Miss Saigon*. I knew she was going to start talking about Mark and Rebecca, so I went into the kitchen. Wellington was there.

'What is wrong?' he asked.

'My mother has invited Mark's parents to lunch,' I said. 'And now she's going to start talking to them about me and Mark.'

Just then, the kitchen door burst open. It was Mum.

'Bridget! What are you doing in here?' she cried.

'Pamela,' said Wellington. 'Do not try and interfere[52] in Bridget's romantic relationships. Now return to your guests and enjoy your lunch.'

Mum doesn't usually listen to anyone. But she was listening to Wellington.

'Well, I suppose you're right,' she said. Then she went back to the dining room.

'Thanks,' I said to Wellington.

'No problem,' he said. Then he added, 'She is a woman with a strong mind and a good heart. But sometimes she has too much enthusiasm[53].'

Later, Mum said, 'I'll give you some food to take back to London. I'll put some things in your bag.' Why does Mum think food is better than love?

Then I went to find my dad.

'You're off back to London?' he said. He gave me a big hug, like he used to[54] do when I was little. It was nice: my dad.

'How have you managed to stay married so long to Mum?' I asked.

'It isn't really so difficult,' he said. He began to sing the words of a Nat King Cole song. *'The greatest thing you'll ever learn is how to love and be loved in return.'*

Then he leaned over and gave me a kiss.

Wednesday 5 March
Weight 9st 2 (good), cigarettes 5 (a pleasant, healthy number), number of phone calls from Mark Darcy 0

8.30 a.m. My flat. I am very sad. I miss Mark. I heard nothing from him all day on Sunday and Monday. Then I got back from work last night to a message saying he was going to New York for a few weeks.

Gaaaaah! Doorbell. Maybe it's Mark coming to say goodbye.

It was just Gary. He came to tell me that the extension to my flat would 'only' cost £7000. He wants £3500 – half the money – now.

£7000. Honestly. Where am I going to get £7000?

Tuesday 18 March
Weight 9st 3, calories 1200, mortgages[55] 2 (hurrah!), number of bedrooms in my flat – about to be 2 (hurrah!)

I rang up my bank and they are going to let me have a second mortgage. I have to fill in a few forms and then they will give me a loan of £7000. I can repay it at the rate of £120 a month. So I have told Gary to go ahead and build the second bedroom and the roof terrace.

I will leave £3500 for Gary in the flat.

Friday 25 April
Weight 9st (yesss! yesss!), cigarettes 4, flats without holes 0, number of pounds in bank 0, boyfriends 0

There is going to be a general election next week. Hopefully Labour will win and everything will become better! I will become better too. I will stop smoking. Mark will come back from New York and find me living in a flat with a second bedroom and a roof terrace.

5.50 p.m. Oh dear. I am worried now about arranging a second mortgage. Perhaps I will not be able to afford to repay it. I'll tell Gary I do not want the extension and get my £3500 back. Gary came round and took the money and left all his tools. But he hasn't started work yet. I will call him when I get home.

6.30 p.m. Back home. Gaaah! Gaaah! Gaaah! There's a great big hole in the side of my flat. There are bricks everywhere.

Saturday 26 April
Weight 9st 4, cigarettes 27 (hurrah!), calories 4248 (hurrah!), gym visits 0 (hurrah!)

6 p.m. A terrible thing has happened. Magda just called.

'Listen, I don't know if I should tell you this, Bridge,' she said. 'Mark's coming home from New York next week and Rebecca's invited us to a welcome back dinner for him.'

I sat down at the kitchen table.

'Oh God,' I said. 'Oh God.'

6.30 p.m. I am going out for cigarettes.

7 p.m. The whole of London is full of couples holding hands in spring. I am going to be alone for the rest of my life. Alone!

Tuesday 29 April

I cannot believe Gary the Builder. I have left him a message every day this week and I have heard nothing from him. No reply. Maybe he's sick or something.

There's also a really horrible smell on the stairs.

There's a great big hole in the side of my flat.

Wednesday 30 April

Hmmm. I just got home from work and the hole has been covered up with a big sheet of polythene[56]. But there is no note, no message, nothing about giving me my £3500 back. Nothing. I wish Mark would ring.

Thursday 1 May

Weight 9st 2, contributions to New Labour victory 0

7.30 p.m. Hurrah! It's election day today. I just got back from the shop. There is a fantastic atmosphere outside.

10.30 p.m. I cannot believe what has happened. I have let down Tony Blair and my country. I went to the voting station but they said I was not registered to vote. They sent me a form to fill in last October, but I didn't open it.

Now I feel terrible. What if we lose the whole election by one vote? It will be my fault, my fault.

Friday 2 May

Weight 9st 1 (hurrah! The first pound lost in the New Labour era)

8 a.m. Hurrah! New Labour has won the election.

Saturday 3 May

Weight 9st 2, cigarettes 5 (very good), calories 1800 (very good), positive thoughts 4 (excellent)

8 p.m. There is a new, positive mood in Britain because of New Labour. I feel positive too. Rebecca is having a dinner party, but that does not mean she is going out with Mark, does it?

8.30 p.m. Hmm. It is not a very nice thought that the dinner party is actually tonight.

10 p.m. I wonder if Magda is back home yet. She promised to call me as soon as she got back and tell me what happened at the dinner party.

11.35 p.m. Magda still hasn't rung. Maybe Rebecca's dinner party is a fantastic success. Maybe Mark is announcing his engagement to Rebecca … Ooh, telephone.

'Hi, Bridge, it's Magda.'

'So how was it?' I asked, too quickly.

'Oh, it was quite nice actually. The food was lovely.'

That was completely the wrong thing to say.

'And how was Mark?' I asked.

'Oh fine,' Magda replied. 'He's a really nice chap, isn't he? Terribly attractive.'

'And do you think he's going out with Rebecca?'

'Hmmm. I'm not sure.'

'Did he mention me?'

'Um. Um. To be honest, Bridge, I don't think he did.'

Monday 5 May
Weight 9st 1 (hurrah!), progress on hole in wall by Gary 0

When I got back from work today, there was a message from Gary. He said he was busy with another job, but he would come round tomorrow night.

Tuesday 6 May
Weight 9st 2, thoughts about Mark – better, progress on hole in wall by Gary 0

7 p.m. I am very depressed. I miss Mark so much. I cannot believe he is going to go out with Rebecca. Obviously there is something wrong with me.

7.30 p.m. Gary is late.

7.45 p.m. There is still no sign of Gary.

8 p.m. There is still no Gary.

8.15 p.m. Gary has not come.

Saturday 10 May
Weight 9st 3, cigarettes 7, calories 3255, positive thoughts 4, progress on hole in wall by Gary 0

11 a.m. I've just been out for cigarettes. It is really, really hot outside.

11.15 a.m. The smell on the stairs is really bad today.

12.55 p.m. Hurrah! I am going swimming at Hampstead Ponds with Jude and Shazzer.

Midnight. We had a very good time swimming at the Ponds. But after we had been swimming, Jude said, 'I've got something to tell you. Vile Richard and I are getting married.'

Shaz and I looked at her in horror. Jude's face turned red.

'I know, isn't it wonderful?' she said. 'Will you two be my bridesmaids[57]?'

Sunday 11 May
Weight 9st 2, cigarettes 15, fantasies about Mark 2 (great)

Shaz just called. We both agreed that Jude must not marry Vile Richard because:
  a) He is mad.
  b) He is vile.
  c) We don't want to have to dress up in pink bridesmaids' dresses and walk down the aisle[58] with everyone watching us.

I called Magda and told her about Jude and Vile Richard.

Then she said, 'Bridget, could you look after Constance, Harry and the baby next Saturday?'

Constance is nearly three, Harry is one and the baby is just a few months old. I have promised to have them while Magda goes to the hairdresser's. Also she and Jeremy are having a party in six weeks' time for Constance's birthday and she asked me if I wanted her to invite Mark. I said yes. You see, he has not seen me since February. It will be good for him to see how much I have changed.

7

At Rebecca's Again

Saturday 17 May

Weight 9st 2, cigarettes 0

I am completely exhausted by my working week. I am almost too tired to get out of bed. Gaaah! Doorbell.

Later. It was Magda with Constance, Harry and the baby. I had forgotten that I had agreed to look after them while Magda had her hair done.

'Here we are!' said Magda, coming noisily up the stairs with a pushchair. 'Ooof. What's that smell? Sorry, but I've got to go. I'm late for the hairdresser's. Everything you need is in the bag under the pushchair.'

I took the children to the park. We had a very nice time. But when we got back and were standing on the pavement outside my flat, Constance was sick all over my hair and the baby started screaming.

'Hello,' said a man's voice. I turned round. Mark Darcy was there, looking confused.

'They're Magda's children,' I said.

'Who's that?' said Constance, looking up at him suspiciously.

'I'm Mark,' he said. 'I'm Bridget's friend. Can I help you upstairs?'

I carried the baby and held Constance's hand, while Mark brought the pushchair and held Harry's hand. Then I heard voices on the stairs. There were two policemen emptying the hall cupboard. They'd had a complaint from the neighbours about the bad smell.

I went upstairs and gave the children a drink. Then one of

the policemen appeared with a holdall bag. It was mine. He pulled a polythene bag of horrible flesh covered with blood from the bag. A terrible smell was coming from the flesh.

The phone rang. It was my mother. Suddenly I remembered something. Mum had given me that bag of food to take back to London after the lunch with Mark's parents. I had left the bag in the hall cupboard.

'Mother,' I said, 'when I came for lunch, did you put any meat in my bag?'

'Yes. Two pieces of steak. In the side pocket,' she said.

'Why didn't you tell me?'

I made my mother explain to the policemen what had happened. They looked at each other. Then they closed their notebooks and went away. Mark stared at the hole in the wall as if he didn't know what to do. Then he suddenly rushed down the stairs after the policemen.

Wednesday 21 May

Weight 9st 1, cigarettes 12 (excellent), calories 3425, progress on hole in wall by Gary 0

Shaz and I went round to Jude's place. There were magazines about weddings everywhere.

'Listen,' said Shaz. 'DON'T MARRY VILE RICHARD. He's selfish and you can't depend on him for anything.'

Jude went all quiet. She breathed in deeply through her nose.

'Let's talk about the bridesmaids' dresses,' she said. 'And there's something I have to tell you, Bridget. Rebecca is bringing Mark to the wedding.'

I looked at Jude. I didn't know what to say.

'And they have asked me to go on holiday with them.'

'What?' shouted Sharon. 'Bridget's your best friend, and Rebecca has stolen Mark. And you're going on holiday with

Rebecca? Well, Jude, if that's the sort of friend you are, you can ask Rebecca to be your bridesmaid, not us!'

So now Sharon and I are not speaking to Jude. Oh, dear.

Sunday 22 June
Weight 9st 3, cigarettes 5 (very good), calories 2455

Yesterday was Constance's birthday party. When I arrived, there were lots of children and adults running around in the garden. Then I saw Mark and Rebecca. Rebecca was kneeling[59] down beside Constance.

Constance smiled and ran towards me. She put her arms round my neck.

'Have you brought me a present?' she asked.

'Yes,' I said. I had brought her a pretty pink dress. She liked it very much and put it on at once.

'Ooh, look, it's a fairy,' said Rebecca, picking Constance up. 'Are you a fairy? Do you live in a fairy castle? Where are your fairy-wairy friends?'

'Bridget,' said Constance. 'Please tell this lady I'm not really a fairy.'

Later, Shaz and I saw Jude across the garden, chatting to Magda. Rebecca went across to talk to Jude.

'Oh, Jude, I'm so happy for you!' she said. Then she turned to Magda. 'Oh, you and Jeremy must come. Bring the children! I love children! It's the second weekend in July. All sorts of lovely people are coming! Jude and Richard, and Mark will be there, and Giles and Nigel from Mark's office …'

'Have you invited Bridget and Sharon?' asked Jude.

'Oh.' Rebecca looked embarrassed. 'Well, I don't think we've got enough room. But perhaps they could stay in the cottage.' She looked round at us. 'You're coming on the twelfth, aren't you?'

'Where?' asked Shaz.

'My parents' place in Gloucestershire. Second weekend in July.'

'We'd love to come,' said Shaz firmly, pressing her foot down on mine. 'Of course we're going,' she said to me when Rebecca had gone. 'You're not going to let her steal *all* your friends, are you?'

'Bridget?' said a voice behind me. I turned to see a short man with red hair and glasses. 'It's Giles, Giles Benwick. Do you remember? You were terribly helpful on the phone that night when my wife said she was leaving.'

'Oh, yes, Giles. How's everything?' I said.

'Not very good, I'm afraid,' said Giles. He started talking about the break-up of his marriage.

Then Magda came over. 'Can you look after Constance for a few minutes?' she said, and she took Giles away.

I knelt down beside Constance. Then Magda came back.

'I think Giles likes you,' she said. Before I could get up, someone started smacking my bottom. It was William, a six-year-old boy. He jumped up on my back and put his arms tightly round my neck.

'Stop it, William,' I said. My back was really hurting. Then suddenly someone pulled William's arms away from my neck. I turned to see Mark Darcy walking away with William under his arm.

Later, Mark came over to me.

'Thank you for helping me,' I said.

'That's OK,' he said. 'I'm, err, going home now. Don't leave with any pieces of meat in your bag, will you?'

Saturday 12 July
Weight 20st 12 (I feel like that, compared to Rebecca)

Rebecca's house, Gloucestershire. I am in the horrible guest cottage. Why did I come here? Why? Shaz and I were late and we arrived ten minutes before dinner. Mark was at the head of the table, sitting next to Rebecca.

'Bridget! Over here!' someone shouted. It was Giles Benwick. I sat between Giles and Magda's husband, Jeremy.

'So! It looks like Darcy's keen on your friend Rebecca!' Jeremy said loudly.

During the meal, Giles kept talking about his marriage. Afterwards, there was dancing. Rebecca was dancing with Mark, her arms round his neck. Then Shaz put on some different music. She took Mark away from Rebecca and started dancing with him instead.

Sunday 13 July
Weight 22st 10, cigarettes 12 (all secret), people rescued from water accidents 1, people who should have been left in the water 1

After breakfast, I decided to walk round the water garden. It was pretty, with small streams and little stone bridges. I sat down in front of a hedge. Then I heard voices on the other side of the hedge. It was Mark and Rebecca.

'My father and mother go everywhere together,' said Mark.

'Oh, I love that!' said Rebecca. 'If I were married to someone I really loved, I would want to be with them all the time.'

'Would you?' he said excitedly. Then he went on. 'But some women don't have room for a man in their lives. Their friends are more important.'

'I love my friends,' said Rebecca. 'But they're not the most important thing for me.'

'And some women believe everything they read in self-help books,' said Mark. 'But self-help books are full of rubbish.'

My heart was beating hard. Was Mark talking about me?

'Oh, I quite agree,' said Rebecca. 'I have no time for all that stuff.'

They went away. I thought about what I had heard.

63

After lunch, everyone sat under a tree at the edge of the lake. There was an old stone bridge over the water. It was very peaceful.

Rebecca suddenly jumped up. 'I'm going to jump off the bridge!' she shouted. 'We used to do it when we were little. It's great fun!'

'But the water's very low,' said Mark.

'I really don't think you should, Rebecca,' said Jude.

But Rebecca took off her shoes and climbed up to the edge of the bridge. Mark got to his feet, looking worriedly at the water and then up at the bridge.

'Rebecca!' he said. 'I really don't think …'

'It's all right,' she said, throwing her hair back playfully. Then she looked upwards, raised her arms and jumped. Everyone stared as she hit the water. She came up again, screaming. Mark rushed towards the lake, went into the water and pulled her out. She limped[60] slowly towards us.

I got the number of her doctor and called him on my mobile phone. The doctor spoke to Rebecca and she moved her foot around according to his instructions. The doctor decided that it was nothing serious – she hadn't broken any bones.

'Where's Giles?' asked Mark. 'I haven't seen him all morning.'

'I'll go and see,' I said.

I went back into the house. It was nice to get into the cool of the entrance hall. 'Giles?' I said. 'Giles?'

There was no reply. I started climbing the staircase. Then I heard a moan[61].

'Giles?' I said. Nothing. 'Giles? It's Bridget.' The moaning noise came again. I walked along the corridor and pushed open the door of a room. Giles was lying on his back with his head turned to one side.

'Bridget.' He was holding a bottle of pills. Temazepam.

'How many have you taken?' I said, taking his hand.

Then she looked upwards, raised her arms and jumped.

'Six … or four. Not long … ago.'

'Make yourself sick,' I said.

We went into the bathroom and I waited while he was sick. Afterwards, I gave him lots of water. He told me he had called his wife and begged her to come back. But she had said she wanted a divorce. He had been so upset that he had taken the temazepam.

Mark appeared in the doorway. I told him what had happened and asked him to ring the doctor again.

'I just want everything to stop,' said Giles.

'No, no,' I said. 'You have to have hope and confidence that everything will turn out all right.'

Mark spoke to the doctor. 'You're going to be all right, Giles,' he said. 'The doctor will be here soon. He said there's nothing to worry about.'

He turned to me. 'You're doing a great job,' he said. 'Will you stay with him till the doctor comes?'

After the doctor had come, I saw Rebecca in the hall talking to Mark. She was crying and sitting with her foot up.

'It's just so selfish of him,' Rebecca was saying. 'It's spoilt the whole weekend.'

After Shaz and I had said goodbye and were putting our bags in the car, Mark came out to us.

'Well done,' he said to me. 'You were great back there, with … well, with both of them.'

As we drove away, I thought about the conversation I'd overheard behind the hedge.

8

The Poetry Evening

Monday 14 July

Weight 9st 4, cigarettes 12, calories 3752, self-help books I am going to throw away 42

8 a.m. I am very confused. Has reading self-help books, which are written to improve my relationship, destroyed my relationship?

8.30 a.m. I have thrown away all my self-help books.

6 p.m. It was a terrible day at work. I don't want to go straight home to my flat with the hole in the wall. It's a beautiful, soft sunny evening. Maybe I will go for a walk on Hampstead Heath.

9 p.m. I was walking on Hampstead Heath. Suddenly I saw a happy-looking couple sitting on the grass. Something about them looked familiar. As I got closer, I saw that it was Jude and Vile Richard. I paused, wondering if I should walk past or go back. Then Vile Richard saw me and said, 'Bridget?' and Jude looked up.

'Hey, it's good to see you, Bridget,' he said with a smile. 'I'm just going to get something to drink. You sit down with Jude.'

When he'd gone, Jude said, 'I missed you.'

Jude apologized for hurting my feelings about Rebecca. She said that she and Vile Richard are not going on holiday with Mark and Rebecca. I said I was sorry for getting angry about something so stupid.

'It wasn't stupid,' said Jude. 'You were really hurt.'

'You really love Richard, don't you?' I said.

'Yes,' she said happily.

Richard came back with a bottle of wine and two packets of cigarettes. I had a lovely evening with them. After I got home, I called Shaz to tell her that I'd seen Jude.

'Oh,' she said when I'd finished speaking. 'Err, Bridge? Do you want to go on holiday? I've found some fantastic cheap flights to Thailand. We could go to the island of Koh Samui.'

'Hurrah!' I said. 'Thailand!'

'Yes,' said Shaz. 'And we're not going to spend time with any men!'

Saturday 19 July

Midnight. I had a lovely evening with Jude and Shaz. It was very nice to be back with the girls again.

My mother rang while I was with them.

'Guess what, Bridget?' she said. 'My friends and I are having a poetry evening a week on Friday. Everyone is going to bring a poem to read and discuss. Will you come?'

'Are Mark's parents coming?' I asked.

'His mother's coming. Mark and his father may come later.'

Friday 1 August
Weight 9st 3, cigarettes 19, calories 625

6.30 p.m. We are leaving for Thailand tomorrow and I haven't packed anything. I didn't realize that the poetry evening is tonight. I really don't want to drive all the way to my parents' village. But I'd better go to support Mum.

Midnight. Just back. Dad and Mark's dad read a poem at the meeting. It was a very famous poem by Rudyard Kipling called *If*. Later, Mark came to take his parents home. As soon as he arrived, he sat down at the table and started writing something.

'Look at Mark, all on his own,' said his father. 'He brought a girl home. What was her name, Rachel, was it?'

'Rebecca,' said Mark's mother.

'And now she isn't here. These young men keep changing girlfriends. I hope you young ladies aren't always running from one boyfriend to another.'

'No,' I said. 'If we love someone, it's hard to forget them when they leave us.'

There was a crash behind me. Mark Darcy had knocked over a glass ornament[62] on the table.

'Are you ready to go, Dad?' asked Mark, looking embarrassed.

Mark and his parents said their goodbyes and left. Suddenly Mark came back and approached me.

'I forgot my pen,' he said. 'When are you going to Thailand?'

'Tomorrow morning.'

'Have you packed?'

'No,' I said.

'Mark,' shouted his father. 'Come on!'

'Coming,' said Mark, glancing over his shoulder. 'This is for you.' He handed me a piece of paper, then left.

I waited, then I unfolded the paper with shaking hands. It was only a copy of the poem *If*. Why did he give me that?

A Nightmare Holiday

Sunday 3 August
Weightless (in air), cigarettes 0 (no smoking in the plane), calories 1 million (because of all the food on the plane)

4 p.m. English time. In an aeroplane in the sky. There's an awful man sitting next to me. He keeps trying to talk to me.

Shaz and I are in separate rows on the plane because we arrived at the airport very late. Now Shaz is sitting next to a man who looks like the actor Harrison Ford. She is chatting to him and laughing at everything he says.

Monday 4 August
Weight 8st 7 (it's not possible to weigh myself here, so I can choose to be any weight I like – excellent advantage of travel), calories 0

2 a.m. local time. Bangkok. It's raining. Shaz and I are in the Sin Sane Guest House. There are no toilets, just holes in the ground. It is awful. The worst thing is that Shaz keeps talking about the man she met on the plane.

'... He's so well travelled ... he tells such interesting and funny stories. He's staying at the Oriental Hotel – he said to come over.'

'I thought we weren't going to spend time with any men,' I said crossly.

'No,' she replied. 'But it's useful to talk to someone who's really well travelled.'

6 a.m. I finally got to sleep at 4.30. My stomach feels very bad.

Noon. Hurrah! We have checked into the Oriental Hotel. It is very expensive, but we can pay by Shaz's credit card. The bathroom is wonderful. I am very grateful that the toilet is so near.

8 p.m. Shaz was asleep so I went out for a walk on the hotel terrace. I stood looking down on the Chao Phraya River. It was beautiful with lots of lights and boats. I was going to light a cigarette when someone held a lighter in front of my face. It was Harrison Ford, the man from the aeroplane. He said his name was Jed.

He asked what our plans were. I told him we had decided to go to Koh Samui. He said he might come too. Then he lifted a finger and touched my cheek. He leaned forward to kiss me.

'Bridget,' said an angry voice. 'I thought you were my friend.'

Oh no, oh no. It was Shaz.

Thursday 7 August
Weight 8st 6 or maybe 2?, cigarettes 10, the number of times the sun has appeared 0

Koh Samui Island, Thailand. We have arrived at a lovely beach, although unfortunately it is still raining. We are staying in one of the beach huts. Things are still cool between Shaz and me.

Friday 8 August
Weight 8st 0, cigarettes 0 (very good)

11.30 a.m. When I woke up, I could not find Shaz. I came outside and looked around. There was a new man in the hut next door. When I looked at him more closely, I saw that it was Jed. He turned round and smiled at someone coming out of his hut.

It was Shaz.

Friday 15 August
Weight 8st 1, cigarettes 25, disasters 1

9 a.m. We have had a fantastic holiday. Shaz was often with Jed, but I swam and sunbathed when they were together. But Jed left last night to visit some other islands. Shaz and I are going to have breakfast now.

11.30 a.m. A terrible thing has happened. When we got back from breakfast, we found that our hut has been broken into[63] and our bags are missing. Our air tickets and money have gone. We only have $38 between us.

5 p.m. I will go to the big hotel near the beach and tell the people there what has happened. I will ask them what to do.

7 p.m. Hurrah! Everything is going to be fine. I met Jed at the hotel. He hadn't gone to the islands because it was too rainy. I told him what had happened. He said he would get us tickets for the train to Bangkok tomorrow. He also gave us money for a hotel in Bangkok and for new air tickets.

Monday 18 August

On the train to Bangkok. I cannot stop thinking about Jed. He was so kind and wonderful. He gave us a new bag to put our stuff in. Shaz is happy because they are going to see each other in London.

Tuesday 19 August

11 a.m. Bangkok Airport. A terrible nightmare is happening. I was carrying our bag in the airport. Shaz had gone on in front and I had to walk past an official with a dog. The dog got very excited and started to bark. Then the airline officials all started talking and an army woman took me into a separate room.

Then the officials emptied my bag, took a knife and cut the lining[64]. Inside was a polythene bag full of white powder.

Wednesday 20 August

11 a.m. I have been arrested by the Bangkok police. I must stay calm. Calm. Calm. Calm. I am in a prison cell.

11.05 a.m. I've realized what has happened. Jed stole all our things, then gave me a bag with drugs sewn into the lining. Anyway, I expect the British Ambassador will be here soon.

Noon. I am getting worried because the British Ambassador is not here.

3 p.m. Maybe no one has told the British Ambassador about me. Where is Shaz? Have they arrested her too?

3.30 p.m. I've got to keep calm … Oh God, I'm so hungry.

4 p.m. The guard just came by with some disgusting rice and some things I was allowed to keep – a photo of Mark Darcy and a bit of paper.

4.30 p.m. Even when things seem bad, good things can still happen. The piece of paper was Dad's poem from the poetry reading. Mark had given it to me that evening.

If by Rudyard Kipling
'If' you can keep your head when all the people round you
Are losing theirs and …

Oh my God. Oh my GOD. Do they cut people's heads off in Thailand?

Then the officials emptied my bag, took a knife and cut the lining.

Thursday 21 August

Weight 5st (very good but imaginary), cigarettes 0, calories 12 (rice)

10 a.m. A young British man in a pink shirt came to see me.

'Are you the British Ambassador?' I yelled.

'Ah. No,' he said in a confident voice. 'I'm Assistant to the Consul. My name's Charlie Palmer-Thompson.' He asked me what had happened and wrote everything down in a notebook. From time to time he said, 'Yar, yar. Oh God, how awful.' But he didn't seem (a) to understand that the situation was serious (b) to be very intelligent and (c) to understand that it was all a mistake.

'Jed must have broken into our hut and stolen our bags,' I said. 'Then he gave us a bag with drugs in the lining. He was using us to take the drugs back to London for him.'

'But if Jed doesn't confess[65],' said Charlie, 'you've got a problem.'

'What will happen to me?' I asked.

'Well,' said Charlie, 'you'll probably go to prison for ten years.'

'TEN YEARS?' I cried. 'But I haven't done anything wrong.'

Charlie said he could make two phone calls for me, to tell people what had happened. I didn't want Mark Darcy to know that I was in trouble again. So I asked Charlie to call Shaz and Jude instead.

Sunday 24 August

Minutes spent crying 0 (hurrah!)

2 p.m. Hurrah! I'm suddenly the most popular girl in the cell. The other women really like Madonna songs and I've been teaching them the words. Then they asked me to sing a

Madonna song. So I jumped up on top of a pile of mattresses[66] and started singing.

Just then the guard brought in Charlie Palmer-Thompson.

'Ah, Charlie,' I said, getting down off the mattresses and hurrying towards him. 'I'm so glad you've come.'

Charlie gave me a box from the British Embassy with water, biscuits, sandwiches, pens and paper, and, best of all, soap.

'Thank you,' I said. 'Now, Charlie ... about Jed.'

Charlie looked at me blankly.

Then suddenly I had an idea. 'What does your father do, Charlie?'

'Oh, he's in the Foreign Office[67],' Charlie replied.

'How's your career going?' I asked.

'Bit slow – to be honest.'

'Well, here's a chance to change that,' I said. 'So why don't you give your dad a call?'

Monday 25 August

6 p.m. Something exciting has happened! An hour ago the guard came and took me out of the cell to a small interview room. A short, middle-aged Thai man came in and introduced himself as Dudwani. Dudwani works for the Drug Squad[68].

I started telling him my story. I gave him a description of Jed.

'So surely you can find him?' I said.

'Oh, we know where he is,' said Dudwani. 'He's in Dubai.'

Suddenly I felt angry.

'Oh, he's in Dubai, is he?' I said. 'And you know all about him. And you know he did it. And you know I didn't do it. So why don't you get him to confess?'

'But he's in Dubai,' said Dudwani.

'Someone must have seen him break into the hut. Someone must have sewn the drugs into the lining of my bag. It was done with a sewing machine.'

Dudwani cleared his throat to speak. 'We ...'

'I am a journalist,' I interrupted him. 'On one of Great Britain's top television programmes,' I said, thinking of Richard Finch. 'I have connections in the highest level of government. And our media will make Thailand look very bad if I am imprisoned here for a crime I did not commit.'

I sat back and gave him a cool stare.

Dudwani looked embarrassed. He looked at his papers then asked, 'Miss Jones, when did you realize your hut had been broken into?'

Hah!

Saturday 30 August
Weight 8st, cigarettes 0, calories 8755 (hurrah!), the number of times I've checked my bag to make sure no drugs are in there 24

6 a.m. I'm on the plane. I'm going home. I'm free! Everything is marvellous.

6.30 a.m. The guards came to my cell last night and called me out. I met an embassy official called Brian. He said there'd been a 'development' in Dubai, and they had to get me out of the country immediately.

Brian took me to the embassy. I had a shower and changed into some clean clothes. Then he took me to the airport.

9 p.m. UK time now. When I arrived at Heathrow, I looked around for people that I knew. Suddenly a crowd of photographers and journalists appeared. My mind went completely blank. I could not think of what to say or do.

Then some people put their arms round me saying, 'It's all right, Bridge, we're here, we've got you, it's all right.'

It was Jude and Shaz.

Sunday 31 August

Weight 8st 2 (Yess! Yess!), calories 8995 (I deserved food, surely, after my time in prison), progress on hole in wall by Gary the Builder 0

2 a.m. My flat. It's so nice to be home and to see Jude and Shazzer again. At the airport, a policeman took us through the crowd to an interview room. There were people from the Drug Squad and a man from the Foreign Office. They asked me lots of questions, then a policeman took us back to my flat.

My friends had filled my fridge with food. There were pizzas and chocolates and bottles of champagne. There was a big sign on the polythene which covered the hole in the wall, saying 'Welcome back, Bridget!'

Jude and Shaz had cleaned up the flat and put clean sheets on the bed and fresh flowers and cigarettes on the bedside table. I love the lovely girls.

10 a.m. Oooh, I've just remembered I'm going to be in the newspapers today. I will go and get them from the shop.

10.30 a.m. The newspapers are full of stories about the death of Princess Diana. Diana and her friend, Dodi Al Fayed, were killed in a car crash in Paris late last night. I cannot believe it.

10

Strange Times

Weight 8st 2 (I must make sure I don't put the weight back on immediately), calories 6452

Shaz, Jude and I were talking about my arrest in Thailand.

'The airline people wouldn't tell me what had happened,' said Shaz. 'They made me get on the plane and they wouldn't let me off again.'

'Jed was waiting at Heathrow,' said Jude. 'But someone at Bangkok Airport told him you'd got arrested. So he immediately got on a plane to Dubai.'

'Jude and I went to the Foreign Office,' said Shaz. 'But they weren't very helpful. So we called Mark and he contacted everyone he knew who might help.'

'We heard you'd been transferred to prison,' said Shaz. 'And Mark got on a plane to Dubai. He was fantastic.'

'He went to Dubai? For me?' I said.

'He's still there,' said Jude. 'Then on Monday we got a call from the Foreign Office. They started being really helpful.'

'That must have been when Charlie talked to his dad!' I said excitedly.

'And then on Tuesday we heard they'd got Jed ...'

'And Mark called on Friday and said they'd got a confession ...'

'Then we got a call to say that you were on the plane!'

'Hurrah!' we all said. I really wanted to talk about Mark.

'Is Mark still going out with Rebecca?' I asked.

'No!' said Jude. 'Rebecca's going out with Giles Benwick now.'

'You know,' said Jude, 'the man who works with Mark, who you rescued from killing himself at Rebecca's ...'

'That's strange,' I said. 'Giles isn't handsome or rich. And he isn't someone else's boyfriend.'

'Yet she has chosen him,' said Shaz. 'It's very strange.'

Tuesday 2 September
Weight 8st 3 (I will definitely stop eating so much tomorrow), cigarettes 27 (I must not start smoking too much), calories 6285 (I must not start eating too much)

It is ridiculous to have a great hole in the wall after four months. I am fed up with Gary the Builder. So I have asked a lawyer friend of Jude's to write him a letter.

Dear Sir,

We are writing to you on behalf of our client, Ms Bridget Jones.

You agreed to build an extension to our client's flat, which would include a second bedroom and a roof terrace. You said this would cost £7000. Our client paid £3500 to you on 21 April 1997.

You began work on 25 April 1997 by knocking a large hole in the wall of our client's flat. You returned on 30 April 1997 and covered the hole with polythene. Since then our client has tried to contact you by telephone. But you have not come back to finish the work or responded to any of her messages.

Unless we hear from you within seven days, we will start legal proceedings[69] against you.

Hah! This will show Gary that I am serious.

Friday 5 September

Weight 8st 7, cigarettes 0

8.20 a.m. Ooh, a package has come for me. Maybe it's a gift!

8.30 a.m. Mmm. It's in a gift box with roses on. Maybe it's from Mark Darcy! Maybe he's back.

8.40 a.m. It looks like a lovely little gold pen with the top cut off. My name is on it. It has a red tip. Maybe it's a lipstick.

8.45 a.m. That is weird. There is no note in there. Maybe it's a lipstick from a company promoting their products.

8.50 a.m. But it is not a lipstick because it is solid. Maybe it is a pen. With my name on it! Maybe it is an invitation to a party – perhaps to celebrate the launch of a new magazine called *Lipstick!*

I think I will go to Coins Café and have a coffee. But not, of course, a chocolate croissant.

9 a.m. I am delighted with the little gift. But I'm not sure it's a pen.

Later. Oh my God. I had just sat down with my coffee and chocolate croissant when Mark Darcy came in. He saw me and came over to my table.

'Hello,' he said. Then, nodding at the gift, he asked, 'What's that?'

I could hardly speak because of love and happiness. I handed him the box.

'I don't know what it is. I think it might be a pen.'

He took the little biro out of the box, turned it round, put it back very quickly and said, 'Bridget, this isn't a pen. It's a bullet[70].'

'Bridget, this isn't a pen. It's a bullet.'

Later still. There was no time to discuss Thailand, Rebecca, love or anything.

Mark put the bullet back in the box.

'Stay here. Don't touch it,' he said. He went out into the street and glanced up and down like a TV detective. 'Come on, Bridget! We're going to the police station.'

We got into his car and he drove off. I started talking very quickly.

'Thank you for the poem,' I said.

'What poem?' he said.

'The *If* poem. Oh God, I'm really sorry you had to go all the way to Dubai, I'm so grateful, I ...'

He stopped at the traffic lights and turned to me.

'Stop talking rubbish, Bridget,' he said gently. 'You've had a big shock. You need to calm down.'

We got to the police station. While we were waiting, Mark made me tell him everything that had happened in Thailand. Then he said, 'Do you think you had better call your boss?'

'Oh, I forgot about work!' I said. By now, it was twenty past ten.

I picked up the phone and dialled Richard Finch's number. I told him someone had threatened to kill me.

'Oooh, that's a good excuse, Bridget,' he said. 'You're at the police station, are you? Have you been taking drugs again?'

That was it. That was enough. I took a deep breath.

'Richard,' I said. 'I don't take drugs. And I'm not coming back. Bye.' I put the phone down. Hah! I thought.

Just then, a policeman rushed by. 'Look!' said Mark. 'This girl has a bullet with her name on. Can someone help us?'

'It's Princess Diana's *funeral* tomorrow,' said the policeman. 'Everyone's very busy.' He went away. Ten minutes later, a detective appeared with a computer printout.

'Hello. I'm Detective Inspector Kirby,' he said, staring at the printout.

'Is that the report about Thailand?' asked Mark, trying to read it over the detective's shoulder.

Just then the phone rang. DI Kirby picked it up. He started discussing the arrangements for Princess Diana's funeral.

'What did the report say about Jed?' I whispered to Mark.

'His real name isn't "Jed",' said Mark. 'It's Roger Dwight.'

DI Kirby put the phone down. 'It looks like Dwight sent the bullet. He wants to punish Miss Jones because he got caught.'

'But Roger Dwight is in prison in Dubai,' said Mark. 'So how could he have organized it?'

The phone rang again.

'Excuse me,' said DI Kirby. He had another long conversation about the funeral.

An hour later, we were still in the police station. The package had been taken away to be checked for fingerprints.

'Is there anyone else who might want to hurt you?' DI Kirby asked me.

'There are lots of people who have hurt me,' I said slowly. 'But I don't think any of them would do this.'

'You're going to have to move out of your flat,' said DI Kirby. 'In case the person tries to kill you. Is there anywhere you can go?'

'You can stay with me,' Mark said suddenly. My heart jumped with excitement. 'In my spare room,' he added quickly.

'Could you leave the room for a moment, sir?' asked the detective.

Mark didn't look very pleased. Then he said, 'Of course,' and went out.

'What exactly is your relationship with Mr Darcy?' asked DI Kirby.

I told him about Mark and me. DI Kirby seemed very suspicious about Mark.

Mark came in again just as he was saying, 'So Mr Darcy just *happened* to be in the café, did he? On the morning you got the bullet?'

'OK,' said Mark. 'Take my fingerprints and give me a DNA test.'

11

At Mark's Place

Friday 5 September, still
*Weight 8st 8, number of seconds I have stayed alive since the death
threat 34 800 (very good)*

6 p.m. Shazzer's flat. It can't be Mark Darcy who wants to kill
me. That's ridiculous. It must be something to do with Jed. I
must keep calm.

I wish Shaz would come back. Her flat is tiny and very
messy. Jude is staying here as well. Everywhere is covered with
bags, boots and clothes.

Saturday 6 September
Weight 8st 9, cigarettes 10, calories 4255

6 p.m. Jude, Shaz and I spent all day watching Princess Diana's
funeral on TV. But I'm feeling a bit lonely now. Jude and
Shaz have gone out. But I'm not allowed to go out without a
policeman to protect me.

Sunday 7 September
*Weight 8st 10, parts of floor not covered by shoes, food, bottles or
lipstick 0*

10 a.m. I was asleep when Jude and Shaz came in last night.
They're still sleeping. Ooh. Telephone. I'd better pick it up so
it doesn't wake them up.

Hurrah! It was Mark Darcy. He said he'd been held at
the police station for seven hours. I told him that it was a bit
crowded in Shaz's flat.

'Well, you can still come and stay with me,' he said casually[71]. 'I've got plenty of bedrooms.'

Just then, Jude turned over and knocked over a pile of shoeboxes with her foot. They crashed to the ground, spilling things into my handbag.

'Thanks,' I whispered. 'I'd love to come.'

11.45 p.m. Mark Darcy's house. Oh dear, things aren't going very well. I am lying alone in a strange room with nothing in it except a bed and a high white chair. Also it's freezing cold.

Mark had to go into work today because he had missed work on Friday. He came home at about 9 p.m. with takeaway food for us both.

I want to tell him how I feel. But if he doesn't want us to get back together, it will be very embarrassing.

Monday 8 September
Weight 8st 11, the number of people sending me death threats whom the police have captured 0 (not very good)

1.45 p.m. I realize I have no job, no money, no boyfriend and a flat with a hole in it. Also, someone wants to kill me. But I'm sure all this is temporary.

2 p.m. I really want my mum.

2.15 p.m. I have called the police and asked them to take me to Debenhams to meet my mum.

Later. Mum was fantastic. We met in Debenhams coffee shop. Mum started talking, but then I started crying.

'Oh, Bridget, Bridget. What's the matter?'

She led me out of the coffee shop and out to the back staircase. We sat down on the stairs and she asked me what was wrong.

Mum doesn't always listen to me. But now she listened to me carefully. When I'd finished, she put her arms round me and gave me a big hug.

'You've been very brave, darling,' she said. 'I'm proud of you.'

It felt so good. At last she stood up.

'Now come along. We've got to think what to do next. I'm going to talk to this detective man. Why haven't the police caught this person yet? You can come and stay with us if you like. But I think you should stay with Mark.'

'But, Mum,' I said. 'Things aren't very good between Mark and me.'

'Listen, darling. If you really love someone, you have to let them know how you feel.'

Tuesday 9 September

2 a.m. In bed, alone. Mark Darcy's house still. When I got home, I felt sleepy and went to bed. I woke up again at midnight.

Maybe I will go downstairs and make myself a cup of tea and watch TV in the kitchen. I keep thinking about what Mum said – that I should tell Mark how I really feel.

8 a.m. I went quietly downstairs towards the kitchen. Suddenly I froze with fear. There was a big shadow ahead of me, moving towards me. I realized it was a man and I started screaming. Then I realized the man was Mark. He was also screaming, even louder than me.

Great, I thought. This is what happens when he sees me with ugly hair and no make-up.

'It's me,' I said. 'It's Bridget.'

Then he sat down on the stairs, shaking. 'Oh,' he said.

He looked so sweet that I sat down next to him, put my arms round him and pulled him close to me.

'Oh God,' he said. 'I feel so stupid.'

Then we both started laughing.

'I thought you were the man who had sent the bullet,' he said.

And then I told him how I felt about him, how I really, *really* felt. And the wonderful thing was, when I had finished, he told me he felt the same.

We went hand in hand down to the kitchen and made some hot chocolate.

'You see,' said Mark, 'when you didn't reply to my note, I thought everything was finished between us.'

'Wait, wait,' I said. 'What note?'

'The note I gave you at the poetry evening, just before I left.'

'But it was just your dad's *If* poem.'

I couldn't believe it. Mark said that when he knocked the ornament off the table, he had been writing me a note. The note said that he still loved me and that I should ring him that night if I felt the same. But in the confusion of knocking over the ornament, he had given me the wrong piece of paper.

Then he said his house was big, cold and lonely without me. And he really liked it best in my flat where it was comfortable and warm. And he said that he loved me and nothing was any fun without me.

The rest of that night was wonderful.

Friday 12 September

It was a wonderful day. Mark and I went to the supermarket and bought food. Later, while we were cooking dinner, the phone rang. Mark answered it and passed it to me.

And then I told him how I felt about him, how I really, really *felt.*

'It's the police,' he said. 'They've got the man who sent you the bullet.'

Mark held my hand as I took the phone, shaking.

'Hello, Bridget, it's DI Kirby here. We're holding a suspect over the bullet. We've obtained a DNA match. The DNA from the stamp on the envelope matches the DNA on a cup in your apartment.'

'Who is it?' I whispered.

'Does the name Gary Wilshaw mean anything to you?'

Gary! Oh my God. 'He's my builder.'

DI Kirby said that Gary was wanted for a number of burglaries. They were keeping him at the police station.

Midnight. My flat. DI Kirby called back half an hour later and said that Gary had confessed.

'It's all over now,' said Mark, holding me and stroking my hair. 'It's all right. Everything's going to be fine.'

12

A Wedding

Saturday 6 December

11.20 a.m. It's Jude's wedding day today. Shazzer and I are bridesmaids. But Shaz isn't feeling very well.

Later. I arrived at the church and looked for Mark. When he saw me in my huge shiny bridesmaid's dress, he looked as if he was going to start laughing. Rebecca was among the guests at the back of the church with Giles. She was wearing a beautiful grey suit and kept looking at Mark.

Shaz and I followed Jude down the aisle of the church, to where Vile Richard was waiting. He looked great. He was just wearing an ordinary suit which was nice – not all dressed up like an actor in a film.

As the vicar was performing the marriage ceremony, Shaz fainted. At once Simon rushed forward. She fell into his arms and he took her away into the vestry, the room in the church where things are stored.

After the marriage ceremony, we all went to the wedding reception. Jude's father is a very rich and successful businessman. So the reception was at Claridge's, a very expensive hotel.

By this time, Shaz was feeling better. While Jude's father was making a speech, I whispered to her, 'What's going on with you and Simon?'

'Nothing,' she said.

After Jude's father had finished his speech, Vile Richard gave a short speech and then Jude stood up. She said a few nice words of thanks and then – hurrah! – she started reading out something that Shaz and I had written with her last night. This is what she said:

'Today I am no longer single. But although I am now a Married, I promise I will never be a Smug Married person. I will never ask any single people "How is your love life?"

'I also promise to keep in close touch with my best friends, Bridget and Sharon. They are the best friends a girl could have in the whole world.'

There was a huge roar of applause[72]. I love Jude, I love Shaz, I thought, as everyone stood up and raised their glasses to us.

'The bridesmaids,' said everyone. It was marvellous having all the attention. I saw Simon smiling at Shaz. When I looked across at Mark, he was smiling at me too.

The rest of the reception was lovely. The best bit was when I went out to the ladies' room. Simon was kissing Shaz in the corridor outside. Sometimes you see relationships starting that you just know are going to work. I knew that this was going to be a very good relationship for Shaz.

I went back into the reception before Shaz and Simon saw me. Suddenly I saw Rebecca talking to Mark. I hid behind a wall and listened.

'Bridget is wrong for you, darling,' she was saying. 'And Giles is wrong for me.'

'But, Rebecca,' said Mark quietly. 'I need Bridget.'

I moved away, smiling. Later I watched Magda dancing with Jeremy. Her head was on his shoulder and her eyes were closed. You can tell they are still very much in love with each other.

I felt someone's hand move round my waist. It was Mark, looking at Magda and Jeremy too. 'Want to dance?' he asked.

Monday 15 December
Weight 9st 3, cards sent 0, presents bought 0

6.30 p.m. Today I received two letters. The first was from Cinnamon Productions, the production company that owns *Sit Up Britain*.

Dear Bridget,

We have been checking staff performance this year on Sit Up Britain. Many of the ideas for our best programmes came from you.

We understand you left your job at Sit Up Britain in September because of a disagreement with Richard Finch. Richard, as you may have heard, was removed from his job at the end of October because of 'personal difficulties'.

We would like to invite you to rejoin the team at Sit Up Britain as Assistant Producer. Please telephone my secretary and make an appointment to discuss this further.

Yours,
Grant E. Pike
Chief Executive, Cinnamon Productions

The second letter was from Gary the Builder in prison.

Dear Bridget,
Sorry about the bullet.
Bridget, it was special between us. I was going to finish your extension when I got some money. Then that letter came from your lawyer and I went a bit crazy.
Sorry again.
Gary

Thursday 18 December

11 p.m. Mark came round this evening.

'Bridget,' he said. 'I've been asked to go to Los Angeles for five months. Will you come with me?'

I thought hard. I thought about Jude and Shazzer, and shopping and coffee.

'Bridget?' he said gently. 'It's very warm and sunny there and they have swimming pools.'

'Oh,' I said.

'I'll wash up,' he said. 'And you can smoke in the house.'

I looked at him, so serious and sweet, and thought that wherever he was, I didn't want to be without him.

'Yes,' I said happily. 'I'd love to come.'

Friday 19 December

11 a.m. Hurrah! It will be fantastic in California, with sunshine and millions of self-help books ... Ooh, good, telephone!

'Err, Bridget, it's Mark.' His voice did not sound good. 'There's been a change of plan. The job in Los Angeles has been cancelled. But there is another job I'm quite interested in and, err, I was wondering ... How would you feel about ...'

'About what?' I asked suspiciously.

'Thailand?'

I think I will just have a little glass of wine and a cigarette.

Points for Understanding

1

1 Where was Bridget's mother going on holiday? Why was Bridget worried about this?
2 Who are these people:
   (a) Mark Darcy (b) Richard Finch (c) Magda (d) Gary Wilshaw?
3 Why did Bridget always answer calls from Shaz and Jude?
4 Who is Giles Benwick? Why did he call and why did Mark want Bridget to talk to him?

2

1 Why was Bridget annoyed with Gary when she came back from work? How did she make him leave?
2 Why did Bridget call Rebecca a 'jellyfisher'?
3 Why was Magda upset when she arrived at Bar 192? How did Bridget make her feel better?
4 Why did Jude say 'JELLYFISH ALERT'?
5 How did Bridget feel about going to the Law Society Dinner? How did she prepare herself for it?

3

1 Why did Mark laugh when he met Bridget outside the Law Society Dinner?
2 What made Bridget think that Rebecca was interested in Mark?
3 Why did Bridget get upset with Mark on the way home?
4 Why did Mark feel things weren't right between Bridget and him at the dinner? What explanation did Bridget give him?

4

1 Why wasn't Bridget pleased that Mark was going to New York?
2 What Valentine's Day surprise did Mark arrange for Bridget? Who gave him the idea for this?
3 Who did Bridget unexpectedly meet at Heathrow Airport? Who was with them?
4 Where did Rebecca invite Bridget and Mark? How did Bridget feel about the invitation? Why did she decide to accept it?

5

1 Who is 'Johnny's boy'? Why did he try to kiss Bridget? What trouble did this cause for her?
2 Which of Bridget's friends gave her the best advice about Mark: (a) Shaz (b) Jude (c) Magda?
3 'I'm really depressed about it, aren't you?' What did Bridget think Mark was talking about? What was he really talking about?
4 In what two ways did Wellington show support for Bridget on the evening of *Miss Saigon*?

6

1 How did Bridget get the money for the extension? Why did she later change her mind about getting the work done?
2 What upsetting news did Magda have for Bridget?
3 What problems did Bridget have: (a) in her building (b) in her flat?
4 What was Jude's news? How did Shaz and Bridget react?

7

1 What was causing the bad smell on the stairs in Bridget's building? How did it get there?
2 Why did Shaz and Bridget stop speaking to Jude?
3 Who did Bridget hear talking behind the hedge? What did she learn about their thoughts and feelings?
4 What happened to: (a) Rebecca (b) Giles at the house party?

8

1 Why did Bridget throw away her self-help books?
2 Why did Bridget change her mind about Vile Richard?
3 Where did Shaz suggest going on holiday?
4 What did Mark give Bridget at the poetry evening?

9

1 Why were things 'cool' between Shaz and Bridget when they arrived on Koh Samui Island?
2 How was Jed responsible for Bridget's arrest?
3 How did Bridget persuade: (a) Charlie (b) Dudwani to help her?
4 Why wasn't there anything about Bridget in the newspapers?

10

1 Who was Rebecca going out with when Bridget returned to the UK? Why did Bridget think this was strange?
2 Why did Bridget decide to send a letter to Gary? Why didn't she write the letter herself?
3 Why was Bridget pleased when she received the gift? Why did she change her mind?
4 Why weren't the police very interested in Bridget's problem at the beginning?

11

1 Why did Bridget decide to go and stay at Mark's house?
2 Why did Bridget want to see her mum? How did her mum help
  her?
3 How did Bridget and Mark get back together again?
4 Who sent the bullet? How did the police find this out?

12

1 Who was getting married? Who were the bridesmaids?
2 What two things did Jude promise never to do?
3 Why did Bridget feel positive about Simon and Shaz?
4 Why did the Chief Executive of Cinnamon Productions write to
  Bridget? What had happened to Richard Finch?
5 How did Bridget feel about going to: (a) Los Angeles (b) Thailand?

Glossary

1 **identified** – *to identify with someone* (page 4)
   to feel that you can understand and share someone else's feelings
2 **heroine** (page 4)
   the main female character of a book, film or play, or a good female character
3 **extension** (page 6)
   an extra room or rooms added to a building
4 **caricaturist** (page 6)
   a *caricature* is a description of a person, place or situation that makes them or it seem silly by emphasizing only some aspects of them. A *caricaturist* is a writer who creates descriptions of this kind.
5 **consul** (page 6)
   a government official sent to live in another country and look after their own country's citizens and business interests there
6 **rival** (page 7)
   a person, team or business that competes with another
7 **election** (page 8)
   an occasion when people can say who they want to represent them, especially in government
8 **divorced** (page 8)
   a *divorced* person is no longer married because the marriage has been legally ended
9 **abandoned** – *to abandon someone* (page 8)
   to leave someone when you should stay with them and look after them
10 **marvellous** (page 12)
   very good
11 **Masai tribesman** (page 13)
   a *tribe* is a large group of related families who live in the same area and share a common language, religion and customs. A man who belongs to a *tribe* is called a *tribesman*. The *Masai* are a *tribe* of people who work as farmers and live in Kenya and parts of Tanzania.
12 **current affairs** (page 13)
   political, social and economic events that are happening now and are discussed in news programmes and newspapers

13 **interrupt** (page 14)
to make something or someone stop for a period of time
14 **attend to** (page 14)
to deal with something or someone
15 **potty** (page 14)
a container that is used as a toilet by young children
16 **smack** (page 14)
to hit someone with your flat hand or with a flat object
17 **vile** (page 14)
very unpleasant
18 **traitor** (page 14)
someone who is not loyal to their friends, family or employer
19 **humph** (page 15)
used for showing that you are annoyed or do not approve of
something
20 **gorgeous** (page 16)
very beautiful
21 **cheat** (page 16)
to have sex with someone who is not your husband, wife or partner
22 **chatted** – *to chat* (page 16)
to talk in a friendly way
23 **panic** (page 17)
a sudden strong feeling of fear or worry that makes you unable to
think clearly or calmly
24 **jellyfish** (page 18)
a soft round sea animal that you can see through
25 **swallowed** – *to swallow* (page 18)
to make a movement in your throat as if you are eating food or
drinking
26 **drill** (page 20)
to make a hole using a special tool or machine
27 **sting** (page 20)
many types of jellyfish *sting* you if you touch them. If an insect,
animal or plant *stings* you, it hurts you by putting poison on or into
your skin.
28 **dropped in** – *to drop in* (page 20)
to make a short visit somewhere
29 **free spirit** (page 20)
someone who lives life the way that they want to and does not care
about rules or customs

30 **glance** (page 22)
to look somewhere quickly and then look away
31 **elegant** (page 24)
an *elegant* person is attractive and gentle in their appearance and behaviour
32 **corset** (page 24)
a stiff piece of underwear worn by women to make their waist look thin
33 **eye shadow** (page 25)
a coloured powder that you can put on your eyelids as make-up
34 **blusher** (page 25)
a pink powder or cream that you can put on your cheeks
35 **vote** (page 26)
to show your choice of a person or your opinion on an issue in an election. Someone who *votes* in an election is called a *voter*.
36 **left-wing** (page 26)
someone who is *left-wing* is considered to have socialist aims and ideas, for example that property, money and power should be shared more equally
37 **principle** (page 26)
a basic belief, theory or rule that has a major influence on the way in which something is done
38 **affair** (page 26)
a sexual relationship between two people, especially when one of them is married to someone else
39 **stainless steel** (page 28)
steel is a strong metal. *Stainless steel* has been treated to stop rust forming on its surface, used for making knives, tools and other things.
40 **detach** – *to detach yourself from someone* (page 29)
to stop being involved in a close or emotional way with someone or something. If someone is *detached*, they do not feel involved with another person.
41 **a week on** (page 32)
if something happens *a week on Friday*, it happens seven days after the next Friday
42 **coincidence** (page 34)
a situation in which separate things happen by chance at the same time or in the same way
43 **make up for** – *to make up for something* (page 35)
to do something good, so that something bad seems less important

44 **tanned** (page 37)

someone who is *tanned* has darker skin than before because of spending time in the sun

45 **Kikuyu** (page 37)

the *Kikuyu* are a tribe of people who work as farmers in the hills in central Kenya

46 **cloak** (page 37)

a long, loose coat without sleeves, that fastens around your neck

47 **dare** – *to dare do something* (page 46)

if you *dare* do something, you are not afraid to do it, even though it may be dangerous or shocking or may cause trouble for you. *How dare you/he/she/they* is used for saying how shocked and angry you are about something that someone has done or said.

48 **familiar** (page 46)

behaving in an informal or friendly way towards someone who you do not know very well, especially in a way that makes them feel that you do not respect them

49 **loyal** (page 49)

willing to support, work for or be a friend to someone, even in difficult times

50 **suspiciously** (page 50)

in a way that shows you think someone has done something wrong. If you are *suspicious*, you believe that someone has probably done something wrong. Someone who the police believe may have committed a crime is called a *suspect*.

51 **faint** (page 50)

the feeling that you are going to be unable to see, feel or think. If someone *faints*, they are suddenly unable to see, feel or think for a short time and usually fall to the ground

52 **interfere** (page 51)

to become involved in a situation and try to influence the way that it develops, although you have no right to do this

53 **enthusiasm** (page 51)

the feeling of being very interested in something or excited by it

54 **used to** (page 51)

used for saying what was true or what happened regularly in the past, especially when you want to emphasize that this is not true or does not happen now

55 **mortgage** (page 52)

a legal agreement in which you borrow money from a bank in order to buy a house

56 **polythene** (page 55)
a strong, light plastic used especially to wrap food in and keep it fresh

57 **bridesmaid** (page 57)
a girl or woman who helps a *bride* before and during her wedding. A *bride* is the woman who is getting married.

58 **aisle** (page 57)
a bridesmaid follows the bride in the church when she walks down the *aisle* – the passage between the rows of seats

59 **kneeling** – *to kneel down* (page 61)
to have one or both knees on the ground

60 **limped** – *to limp* (page 64)
to walk with difficulty because of an injured leg or foot

61 **moan** (page 64)
a long low sound that you make because of pain or sadness

62 **ornament** (page 69)
a small attractive object used for decoration or for making someone or something more beautiful

63 **broken into** – *to break into something* (page 72)
to enter a building by force, especially in order to steal things. It is a crime to *break into* a building, and this crime is called *burglary*.

64 **lining** (page 73)
a piece of material that is attached to the inside of something such as clothes, bags or curtains to make them warmer or thicker

65 **confess** (page 75)
to admit that you have committed a crime

66 **mattress** (page 76)
the part of a bed made of thick soft material that you put on the bed's base to make it more comfortable

67 **Foreign Office** (page 76)
the British government department that deals with Britain's relations with foreign countries. Its full name is the *Foreign and Commonwealth Office*. People who represent their government in a foreign country work in an *embassy*. The highest person in an embassy is called an *ambassador*. People with important positions in this and similar organizations are also called *officials*. The police or people in organizations with legal power to make people obey laws or rules are often called *the authorities*.

68 **Drug Squad** (page 76)
the part of the police force whose job is to try to stop the trade in illegal drugs

104

69 **legal proceedings** (page 80)
   the actions taken, usually in court, to settle a legal matter
70 **bullet** (page 81)
   a small piece of metal that is shot from a gun and causes serious damage to the person or thing it hits
71 **casually** (page 87)
   in a way that shows you do not have strong feelings or emotions
72 **applause** (page 93)
   the sound made by people clapping, usually after a performance or a speech

Definitions adapted from the Macmillan English Dictionary 2nd Edition © Macmillan Publishers Limited 2007
www.macmillandictionaries.com

Exercises

Background Information

Put the following events in the life of Helen Fielding, the author of *Bridget Jones: The Edge of Reason*, in order. Use the letters A–J.

1 Helen finished her education and started working as a journalist.	
2 This sequel, *Bridget Jones: The Edge of Reason*, was published.	
3 Helen Fielding was born in 1958.	A
4 Helen created the character of Bridget Jones for the newspaper column.	
5 Helen's newspaper column was turned into a book, *Bridget Jones's Diary*.	
6 Helen was asked to write a newspaper column about herself.	
7 *Bridget Jones: The Edge of Reason* was made into a film.	
8 Helen went to Wakefield Girls' High School.	
9 Helen's first novel, set in Africa, was published.	
10 Helen went to the University of Oxford to study English.	

Multiple Choice

Tick the best answers. Sometimes there is more than one answer.

1 Which of the following facts are NOT true about Rebecca?
  a She had never invited Bridget and her friends on her house-party weekends.
  b She told her nephew that Mark was going to leave Bridget.
  c She broke her leg when she jumped from a bridge. ✓
  d She had never been skiing. ✓

2 Why did Mark tell Bridget that she was doing a great job on the second weekend at Rebecca's parents' house?
  a Because she was looking after Magda's daughter, Constance.
  b Because she had helped Giles and Rebecca.
  c Because she had thrown away her self-help books.
  d Because she had helped Shaz and Magda.

3 How did Bridget become popular with the other women in the Thai prison?
  a She gave them soap and food.
  b She taught them the words to Madonna's songs.
  c She asked Charlie to help them.
  d She played western songs on the guitar.

4 Why did Bridget stay at Mark's house after someone had tried to kill her?
  a Because the police told her not to stay in her own flat.
  b Because her parents were on holiday.
  c Because Jude didn't want her to stay on her own.
  d Because there wasn't enough space in Sharon's flat.

5 Which couples were together at the end of the story?
  a Shaz and Simon, Rebecca and Mark, Richard and Jude
  b Shaz and Simon, Bridget and Mark, Giles and Jude
  c Bridget and Mark, Shaz and Richard, Jude and Simon
  d Bridget and Mark, Shaz and Simon, Richard and Jude

6 Who did Bridget receive letters from at the end of the story?
  a Gary and Mark
  b Giles and a Chief Executive
  c A Chief Executive and Mark
  d A Chief Executive and Gary

Vocabulary: Verbs and nouns

Match a verb with a noun to make phrases from the story.

1	achieve	a loan
2	put on	goals
3	pour	a cigarette
4	repay	make-up
5	play	a hole
6	drill	an answer phone message
7	roll	a glass of wine

Now choose a phrase to complete the sentences below, changing the tense or form of the verbs where necessary. Each phrase may only be used once.

1 Bridget washed her hair, _____*put on make-up*_____ and black jeans to look nice for Mark.

2 Bridget pressed the button to _____ , hoping that it would be from Mark.

3 Gary told Bridget that if he _____ in the wall to put up shelves, the electricity would go off.

4 Magda arrived at Bar 192 and Bridget immediately _____ for her.

5 Gary started _____ , then left Bridget's flat before smoking it.

6 Bridget had to _____ of £7000, which she borrowed to pay for her extension.

7 Bridget made a list of things she wanted to do when Mark was away, but she wasn't very successful at _____ .

Vocabulary: Crime and the police

Complete the gaps. Use each word in the box once.

> cell   burglaries   ~~arrested~~   confessed   protect
> captured   suspect   bullet

1   When Bridget was found with drugs sewn into the lining of her bag, she
    was _____*arrested*_____ and put in a prison _____ .

2   When Bridget received a package, Mark told her it was a _____
    and she realized that someone was threatening to kill her.

3   The police held Gary as a _____ when his DNA matched the
    DNA on the stamp of the envelope.

4   Gary was already wanted by the police because of _____ he had
    committed.

5   Gary admitted that he was guilty. In other words, he _____ to
    the police.

6   Bridget was not allowed to go out without a policeman to
    _____ her until the police had _____ the person who
    had sent her a death threat.

Vocabulary: People

Complete the gaps. Use each word in the box once.

> vicar   ambassador   traitor   ~~boss~~

1   Richard Finch was Bridget's _____*boss*_____ .

2   Bridget felt guilty about not seeing her single friends when she had a
    boyfriend. She felt like a _____ in a war.

3   After her arrest, Bridget started to worry when the British
    _____ did not arrive to help her.

4   A _____ performed Jude's marriage ceremony in church.

Grammar: Past simple and past continuous

Choose the correct tense, past simple or past continuous, to complete the sentences.

1   When Bridget (answered) / was answering the phone, Jude
    cried / (was crying) on the other end.

2   Richard Finch had / was having a meeting with his team when Bridget
    finally arrived / was arriving at work.

3   Bridget saw / was seeing Mark and his friends waving at her because she
    didn't wear / wasn't wearing skis.

4   When Bridget found / was finding Giles, he held / was holding a bottle
    of pills.

5   Bridget walked / was walking through Bangkok Airport when the dogs
    started / were starting barking at her.

Grammar: Reporting verbs

Rewrite the first sentence using the reporting verb given in the second
sentence. Change direct into indirect speech.

> **Example** 'Please don't go to Africa,' said Bridget's father to his wife.
> Bridget's father asked _his wife not to go to Africa_ .

1   'You should go to the ladies' room and look at your face,' said Mark to
    Bridget.
    Mark told ....

2   'I'll build you an extension,' said Gary to Bridget.
    Gary offered ....

3   'Please come back to me,' said Giles Benwick to his wife.
    Giles Benwick begged ....

4 'I'll keep in touch with my best friends, Bridget and Sharon,' said Jude.
  Jude promised ....

5 'I won't be a Smug Married person,' said Jude.
  Jude promised ....

Grammar: Third conditional forms

Rewrite the two sentences in the third conditional. Say what would/ wouldn't have happened if things had been different.

> **Example** A player was sent off. We lost the game.
> If a player *hadn't been sent off, we wouldn't have lost the game* .

1 Bridget's mother went to Africa. She brought back Wellington.
  If Bridget's mother ....
  ....

2 Rebecca was beautiful. Bridget worried about her stealing Mark.
  If Rebecca ....
  ....

3 Shazzer met Jed on the plane. Bridget was arrested in Thailand.
  If Shazzer ....
  ....

4 There were drugs in Bridget's bag. The dog at the airport barked at her.
  If there ....
  ....

5 Mark went to Dubai. The police got a confession from Jed.
  If Mark ....
  ....

6 Jude got married. Bridget and Shazzer were bridesmaids.
  If Jude ....
  ....

Published by Macmillan Heinemann ELT
Between Towns Road, Oxford OX4 3PP
A division of Macmillan Publishers Limited
Companies and representatives throughout the world
Heinemann is the registered trademark of Pearson Education, used under licence.

ISBN 978–0–2304–0022–1
ISBN 978–0–2304–0023–8 (with CD edition)

This version of *Bridget Jones: The Edge of Reason* by Helen Fielding was
retold by Anne Collins for Macmillan Readers.

First published 2010
Text © Macmillan Publishers Limited 2010
Design and illustration © Macmillan Publishers Limited 2010
This version first published 2010

All rights reserved; no part of this publication may be
reproduced, stored in a retrieval system, transmitted in any
form, or by any means, electronic, mechanical, photocopying,
recording, or otherwise, without the prior written permission of
the publishers.

Illustrated by Gavin Reece
Cover by Macmillan Publishers Limited/Dean Ryan

Printed and bound in Thailand
without CD edition
2015   2014   2013   2012   2011   2010
10   9   8   7   6   5   4   3   2   1

with CD edition
2015   2014   2013   2012   2011   2010
10   9   8   7   6   5   4   3   2   1